JAKE THE FAKE

KEEPS HIS COOL

CRAIG ROBINSON   ADAM MANSBACH

ART BY KEITH KNIGHT

CROWN BOOKS
for YOUNG READERS
NEW YORK

I dedicate this book to all those striving to be the best
version of themselves, while seeing the greatness in others.
—C.R.

For Jamie, Viv, Zanthe, and Asia
—A.M.

Dedicated to my two sons, Jasper and Julian,
who have literally grown up with Jake!
—K.K.

Text copyright © 2020 by Craig Robinson and Adam Mansbach
Cover art and interior illustrations copyright © 2020 by Keith Knight

All rights reserved. Published in the United States by Crown Books for Young Readers, an imprint
of Random House Children's Books, a division of Penguin Random House LLC, New York.

Crown and the colophon are registered trademarks of Penguin Random House LLC.

Visit us on the Web! rhcbooks.com

Educators and librarians, for a variety of teaching tools, visit us at RHTeachersLibrarians.com

Library of Congress Cataloging-in-Publication Data
Names: Robinson, Craig, author. | Mansbach, Adam, author. | Knight, Keith, illustrator.
Title: Jake the fake keeps his cool / Craig Robinson, Adam Mansbach; art by Keith Knight.
Description: First edition. | New York: Crown Books for Young Readers, [2020] |
Series: Jake the fake | Audience: Ages 8–12. | Audience: Grades 4–6. | Summary: "Jake loses his
cool when he learns he's about to become the middle child, and he's back to his fakester ways when
new girl Bailey starts school and he'd do anything to impress her"—Provided by publisher.
Identifiers: LCCN 2019052356 (print) | LCCN 2019052357 (ebook) |
ISBN 978-0-553-52359-1 (hardcover) | ISBN 978-0-553-52360-7 (library binding) |
ISBN 978-0-553-52361-4 (ebook)
Subjects: CYAC: Family life—Fiction. | Pregnancy—Fiction. | Schools—Fiction. |
Comedians—Fiction. | African Americans—Fiction. | Humorous stories.
Classification: LCC PZ7.1.R6364 Jag 2020 (print) | LCC PZ7.1.R6364 (ebook) | DDC [Fic]—dc23

Printed in the United States of America
10 9 8 7 6 5 4 3 2 1
First Edition

CHAPTER 1

Tonight, my parents and my sister, Lisa, and I went out for sushi. We've been doing that more and more, because it's the only food we all agree on 100 percent of the time. That means we don't have to stand around our kitchen getting hungrier and hungrier and less and less agreeable and having conversations like:

Mom: How about Indian?

Lisa: No, I'm not in the mood for Indian.

Dad: Italian?

Me: They gave us orecchiette with broccoli rabe at school today.

Dad: Man, that fancy

Lisa's MOOD RING determines WHAT FOOD she'll eat

GREEN: vegetarian

BLUE: seafood

RED: spicy

PURPLE: INDONESIAN

MAGENTA: senegalese

ORANGE: junk

1

art school of yours sure is something! When I was your age, school lunch was—

Me and Lisa and Mom together: Cardboard-and-paste sandwiches.

Dad (pretending we didn't just say the thing he always says, and that it is somehow still funny): Cardboard-and-paste sandwiches! Haha! Okay, how about . . . Senegalese?

Mom: Clarence, the Senegalese place closed. Remember?

Dad: Right. Right. Shucks. I was really in the mood for Senegalese.

Me: Pizza?

Lisa: Pizza is Italian. We already said no Italian.

Me: I meant, like, no pasta, because we had pasta for lunch. I'd eat pizza.

Lisa: I wouldn't. It's just bread and cheese and sauce.

Me: That's like saying the Eiffel Tower is just bricks and cement.

Lisa: The Eiffel Tower is made of metal, doofus.

Me: *You're* made of metal.

Dad: We could just stay home. There's plenty of cereal. It's not just for breakfast, you know. It's delicious anytime.

FUN (fake) FACT:

ALTHOUGH barely noticeable in pictures, THE Eiffel Tower is actually made of fresh baguettes!!

Sometimes I think my dad is secretly a highly paid lobbyist for the Cereal Council of America.

Lisa: Um . . . Korean barbecue?

Mom: Aren't you a vegetarian, Lisa?

Lisa: Oh, yeah.

Dad (hopefully): Wing Ding Doodle?

At some point, my dad always brings up Wing Ding Doodle, which is a wing place he used to go to in college, and which my mom calls Wing Ding Doo-Doo. You know those health-inspection ratings that restaurants are supposed to post on the front window? Wing Ding

Doodle has a D—which does not, as my dad claims, stand for Delicious. It basically means that the rats and cockroaches and badgers infesting the kitchen are on strike until they can get cleaner working conditions.

I would sooner eat a bucket of drool than go to Wing Ding Doodle. I'm not sure whether my dad suggests it because he authentically believes that one of these days we might

agree to eat there, or because he doesn't even want to eat there himself and just does it out of loyalty to his younger self, or because he knows bringing it up is the cue for one of us to say:

Me: How about sushi?

Mom: Sure.

Dad: Great.

Lisa: Rad. I'll go get my wig.

MOZART WIG

THE "BETTY"

B-DAY WIG

THE "MARGE"

ALIVE!!

1:53

Lisa needs a wig because when she doesn't wear one, people sometimes come up and ask for autographs. This is because my sister is famous-ish. She and her boyfriend, Pierre, have this conceptual art band called Conceptual Art Band, and they have had two giant hits in the past three months. One is called "The Ballad of the Duck-Billed Platypus," and the video features

BILLBOARD TOP 3

1. Happy Birthday song
2. The A-B-C song
3. The Ballad of The Duck-Billed Platypus!!
4. National Anthem

FUN (Fake) Fact: 42 OUT OF 45 U.S. PRESIDENTS wore WIGS WHILE in office!!

And TWO were actual WHIGS!!

I love your new WHig!!

Thanks!

me and my best friend, Evan, waddling around in egg costumes. It has gotten something like 300 million views on YouTube. That's the equivalent of every single person in America watching it once. Or every person in France watching it five times. Or every person in my homeroom watching it twenty-five million times.

Their second hit song is called "The Schlemiel and the Schlimazel." It's about one-tenth as successful, which is still pretty good. *Schlemiel* and *schlimazel* are Yiddish words that were taught to me by my comedy mentor, the some-what-legendary and

DUCK-BILLED PLATYPUS

3 millionth Time
24,477,097TH Time
5,700,311TH Time
4,000,188TH Time

usually ornery Maury Kovalski. According to him, the schlemiel is the guy who spills the soup, and the schlimazel is the guy it lands on. If there's a place in Maury's world for a guy who neither spills nor gets soaked in soup, I haven't heard about it.

I should also ask Maury what the word is for a guy who spills soup on himself, since as soon as our nice hot bowls of miso soup got to the table, I managed to do exactly that.

"So . . . ," my mom said after I'd cleaned myself up and the rest of the food had arrived. "You kids might have noticed that I haven't been eating sushi lately."

"Huh?" I said like a goon, stuffing a piece of salmon into my mouth.

"You're eating sushi right now," said Lisa from underneath a short pink bob that made her look like she'd fallen headfirst into a vat of highlighter ink. She was also wearing furry fingerless gloves, a T-shirt with "World's Greatest Grandpa" written in puffy letters across the front, and cutoff turquoise sweatpants. On most people, the outfit would have said "escaped mental patient," but on

I prefer "Robert" to "Bob"!!

8

Lisa it said "rock star," just like everything else she had ever worn in her life.

"This is a California roll," my mother said. "It's cooked."

"Sushi doesn't have to be raw," I said. "What's important is the culinary technique. It may surprise you to learn that many sushi chefs say the single most difficult item to prepare is *tamago*, the sweet egg omelet." I had seen that in a documentary I watched because I couldn't find the remote control and was too lazy to get up and change the channel.

"Did you just say 'culinary technique'?" asked Lisa.

"I did."

"Very impressive." She offered me a palm, and we high-fived.

My parents exchanged another significant look, and my dad said, "There is a reason your mother isn't eating any raw fish."

Lisa stopped chewing. Like, she just sat there with a half-chewed lump of mackerel nigiri in her mouth.

That's when I knew something major was going on.

"No way," said Lisa through the mackerel.

"Yup!" my father replied, nodding enthusiastically.

"You've *got* to be kidding me," said Lisa.

I had no idea what was happening. What could it mean that my mother wasn't eating raw fish, and why would Lisa care?

Acting with the type of quick thinking and poor deductive reasoning for which I am known, I came to an immediate and totally wrong conclusion.

"You have a rare medical condition that makes your mouth so hot it cooks whatever you put in it, so eating raw fish is pointless," I said, nodding like I knew all about it.

"No, dummy," said Lisa. "She's pregnant."

"Holy moly," I said, dropping my chin into my hands and my elbows onto the table. Or, more accurately, one elbow onto the table and the other into my replacement bowl of miso soup, which flipped over and sent a waterfall of soup cascading into my lap. But I was so flabbergasted I barely noticed, except for the intense, scorching pain.

"A baby," I said as the soup quickly cooled. Within a few seconds,

I no longer felt like I had just peed in my pants. Instead, I felt like I had peed in my pants a few hours earlier.

"A baby!" my mother repeated, and she looked so happy and excited that for a second, I felt those things, too. I glanced around the table and saw the same expression on my dad's face and on Lisa's.

"Awesome!" Lisa shouted, jumping up and throwing one arm around my mom and the other around my dad and kissing one and then the other on the cheek.

I didn't want to ruin this moment for anybody, so I smiled as big and bright as I could, and then I jumped

up and hugged both of my parents, and then Lisa and I hugged, too. By the time we all sat back down, everybody was glowing with joy. The food probably would have gotten cold, except that it was cold to begin with.

We all tore back into our sushi, as if this announcement had been some kind of grueling twelve-hour hike that had left us famished. Except for me. My appetite was nowhere to be found, and all kinds of thoughts and feelings were bouncing around inside my mind and stomach like pinballs.

CAN YOU FIND JAKE'S APPETITE IN THIS PICTURE?

ANSWER: NO

The truth was, a new baby was not exactly at the top of my Christmas list. I'm not saying I was absolutely 100 percent against the idea, but my thoughts were a lot more complicated than I wanted to let on right there and then, with everybody celebrating and rejoicing and balloons and confetti practically falling from the ceiling of Osaka City Sushi.

So I said "Awesome" a bunch of times, but really my thoughts were all jumbled up and anxious because:

The official™
Jake le Fake
X-MAS LIST!!
1. WhiRLeD PEas
2. A WeeKeND-
LoNg gig aT THe
CHUcKLe HUT
3. LibraRY CarD
4. SoCCeR goaLie
gLoves
1268. A NeW
BabY SibLiNg

1. **A baby meant I would be the middle kid.** Can you name some notable middle kids throughout history? Of course you can't, because there are none. Middle kids exist for one reason and one reason only: to be ignored. Oldest kids have a role: they're the pioneers, the first to do everything. They break in the parents. In royal families, they get the crown. And once you're the oldest, you're always the oldest. Nobody can take that away from you.

14

Famous Older Children

Infamous Middle Children

OPRAH

J.K. ROWLING

ALL COCKROACHES

weird, huH?

Beyoncé

HILLARY CLINTON

THE POOP emoji

I STILL keep my spirits up!!

Meanwhile, youngest kids are everybody's favorite. They're the precious babies who everybody looks out for, the ones who reap the benefits of their parents being all mellow and relaxed by the time they're teenagers and get away with murder. But middle kids? Middle kids just take up space. They're the lettuce in the family sandwich. Have you ever heard anybody mention the lettuce?

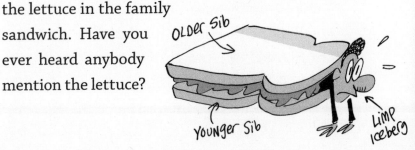

OLDer Sib

YOUNGer Sib

LIMP Iceberg

STUFF BABIES CAN'T DO (It's a LOT!)

Can't fly a fighter jet

What time is it?

Goo?

Can't tell time

Can't fry an egg over-easy

2. **Babies are boring**. Sure, they might be cute—although not always, because some babies look like wrinkled old men, and half the time when people coo and fuss over how cute a baby is, it's only because "Wow, what an ugly baby" is an inappropriate thing to say. But you know why babies are cute? Because evolution had to figure out a way for their parents not to lose interest and wander away. I mean, what do babies do? I'll tell you what: they pee. Also, they poop. They do not do either of these things in a bathroom. If that's not thrilling enough for you, check this out: they also eat. And sleep. And cry. And throw up on a semi-regular basis. They do not become interesting for YEARS, if they ever become interesting at all. No baby has

ever dunked a basketball. No baby has ever built a medieval siege weapon such as a catapult or trebuchet. No baby has ever said anything hilarious. The best you can hope for from a baby, humor-wise, is maybe a well-timed fart. And even that is a stretch. Not to mention stinky.

3. **There are only three bedrooms in our house:** my parents', Lisa's, and mine. Which one of us do you think is going to end up getting the short end of the stick and sharing a room with Li'l Stinky McStinkface? Yup. Ol' Whatshisname, that kid who nobody can even remember anymore because NOW HE'S THE MIDDLE KID.

Obviously, I couldn't say any of this—not when we were celebrating the glorious news and everything. Instead, I pretended to be thrilled, hoping that if I tried hard enough, I might even convince myself.

I also recovered enough of my appetite to eat a gigantic green tea ice cream sundae for dessert. Which was kind of heroic, if you think about it, but don't think about it too hard.

CHAPTER 2

As soon as I stepped into homeroom the next morning, my friend Azure ran up to me with a look on her face like she had just seen a kitten get punched in the nose.

"What's wrong?" she asked. "Jake looks awful."

One of the nice things about friends is that they can see right through you. Of course, one of the problems with friends  is also that they can see right through you.

I heaved a giant sigh.

"My parents are having a baby," I said.

Azure's eyes widened, and so did the spiderwebs drawn around them in eyeliner, which I guess meant that Azure had gotten sick of the Hipster Hillbilly look she'd been into for the past few weeks and was now back to being Goth. "Jake's parents are having a baby," she said.

"Who are you talking to?"

"Who is *Jake* talking to?"

"I'm talking to you."

"*Jake* is talking to *Azure*."

"Why are you—" I stopped short, realizing what was going on. Today was Thursday, and Mr. Allen had announced last week that every Thursday would be Third-Person Thursday and we weren't allowed to say "I" or "me" or "you."

What was educational about that, I had no idea. My friend Forrest, who'd been homeschooled at his family's farm until this year and liked to stuff leaves down his pants so he could feel at one with nature, had asked. Mr. Allen's answer was "It forces the brain

to experience a level of subjectivity that dislocates us from our comfort zones. In other words, it jangles the bangles, Spangles." We all just nodded. Since then, we'd been calling Forrest Spangles, which he seemed to like.

"So is Jake excited?" Azure said. "Because Jake doesn't look excited. Jake looks like someone is forcing Jake to wear a necklace made of moist cat poops."

"Jake is a little bit excited," I said. "But mostly Jake is happy with Jake's family as Jake's family is, and is worried that a baby is going to screw everything up." I had to admit, there was something about third person that made saying all that stuff easier. Like I was talking about a friend instead of myself.

Azure nodded. "Azure understands," she said. "Azure remembers when her sister Cassie was born. When Cassie didn't sleep, nobody slept. And Cassie didn't sleep for two years."

"Jake likes sleep," I said. "No sleep makes Jake go crazy."

"No sleep makes all human beings go crazy," Azure pointed out. "Does Jake know if it's a boy or a girl?"

"Jake doesn't," I said. "But both are bad. If it's a girl, Jake is outnumbered. And if it's a boy, Jake's not special anymore."

"Jake should look on the bright side," said Azure, patting me on the shoulder. "Jake's parents will be so busy with the baby that Jake will be able to do whatever he wants."

STUFF JAKE CAN **FINALLY** TRY NOW THAT HIS PARENTS WILL BE SO **BUSY**

PLAY IN TRAFFIC

Big Cat Dentistry

I knew Azure was trying to make me feel better, but the thought of my parents not having any time to spend with me wasn't as appealing as she seemed to think. In fact, it made me feel a lot worse. Call me a weirdo, but I actually like hanging out with my parents.

Just then, the bell rang, signaling the beginning of homeroom. The bell was a cowbell, and Mr. Allen was wearing it around his neck. He only did that on special occasions, so we all looked up at him right away, wondering what was going on.

"Today is a very exciting day," he said with a big smile, and I noticed he was also wearing a paper party hat with the plastic chinstrap, only he was wearing it upside down, with the strap over his head, so that the hat looked like a pointy beard.

"Today we welcome a new sheep into our little flock," he went on. I guess Third-Person Thursday didn't apply to Mr. Allen.

"Yes!" shouted Forrest, jumping up and pumping his fist. "Finally!"

Klaus, the German exchange student who doesn't play drums in our no-instruments band Crazy American People Who Do Not Make Any Zense (which Klaus also named), rolled his eyes. "Even Klaus know zees eez just expression, Schpangles. Eez not a real zheep."

"Oh," said Forrest, sitting back down.

Mr. Allen smiled in the direction of Hotch, the class snake, and that was when I noticed a girl I'd never seen before standing behind Hotch's glass terrarium.

A really pretty girl, with bangs falling over one eye, wearing a T-shirt that said SPORTS! and a long skirt made of different-colored patches.

"Class, this is Bailey," said Mr. Allen, and the girl strolled out from behind the terrarium and gave us a casual little wave.

"Yo," said Bailey. "I'm Bailey."

Mr. Allen cupped his palm over his mouth and stage-whispered, "Third-Person Thursday!" at her.

"Bailey is Bailey," Bailey corrected herself.

"Tell us a little bit about yourself," Mr. Allen said. "Or tell yourself a little bit about us, if you prefer."

Bailey raised her eyebrows at us, like *Is this guy for real?* and everybody laughed. She seemed really comfortable up there, considering she didn't know anybody and all that.

"Well," said Bailey, "Bailey just moved here, which makes this the sixth place Bailey has lived. Bailey's mother was a chef for the army, so Bailey has lived in Japan, Germany, Florida, Alabama, and San Diego. But now Bailey's mother is opening her own restaurant, and Bailey's dad grew up around here, so here Bailey is. Um . . . what else does the class want to know about Bailey?"

Bin-Bin raised her hand.

Bailey pointed at her. "Yes . . . uh, girl with her hand raised."

"Bin-Bin is Bin-Bin," said Bin-Bin. "What does Bailey like to make, or play, or . . . do?"

Mr. Allen stepped in. "I think what Bin-Bin wants to know is what attracted you to Music and Art Academy."

Bailey counted on her fingers. "Bailey makes wigs. Bailey plays hip-hop accordion— actually, Bailey *invented* hip-hop accordion. Bailey has a black belt in kung fu." She paused for a second. "Bailey also loves the giant squid, and Bailey hates Third-Person Thursday."

"So does Jake," I blurted out. She smiled at me, and I smiled back and felt a kind of charge shoot through me, like I had just picked up an electric eel. Something weird was happening. I'd never had a crush before, but I was pretty sure I had one now. The main feeling was sweat. Sweat and wanting Bailey to smile at me again.

"In honor of Bailey's first day," Mr. Allen said, "we will postpone the start of our new Art and Criticism

unit so we can chat with her a little bit. And as an additional treat . . ." He wiggled his eyebrows and tossed a stack of party hats at Whitman, who didn't react at all because he never reacts to anything. The party hats fell to the ground. Whitman stared down at them the way a goat might stare at a nuclear submarine.

". . . I brought gluten-free, sugar-free vegan cupcakes!" Mr. Allen finished. With a flourish, he reached into his shoulder bag and removed a big box from the Fakery, which is a bakery that refuses to use any of the ingredients that make baked goods good. We think Mr. Allen is their only customer.

"Is this going to be on the test?" asked Cody, who is always worried about the test and doesn't seem to accept that there has never been, and probably never will be, a test.

"Definitely," said Mr. Allen, which is what he always says to Cody. He opened the box, and the smell of fake cupcakes wafted across the room, which until then had mostly smelled of Hotch the snake. I wouldn't say it was an improvement.

A few people wandered half-heartedly in the direction of the cupcakes, and the rest wandered toward Bailey. I wanted to get to her first, so I broke into a kind of cool half jog, which stopped being cool when I failed to slow down fast enough and bumped into Azure, who bumped into Forrest cupcake-first and got vegan frosting all

MORE SPIFFY MR. ALLEN SAYINGS!!

WHAT's swervin' Mervin?

What's shakin', Bacon?

Toodles, my noodles!!

28

over his shirt. Luckily it was Forrest, so he didn't make a big deal about it, just took off the shirt and licked the frosting. Then he said, "Hmm . . . good," walked over to the cupcakes, picked one up, and smeared the frosting all over his shirt.

"That was unexpected," Bailey said, watching him.

"This is a pretty weird place," I said. "Jake would be happy to show Bailey the ropes."

She smiled at me, but it was quicker this time, almost like a tick. "Bailey is pretty used to new schools. She usually just—"

Out of nowhere, Klaus poked his head into the conversation. "Klaus can show ze ropes!" he yelled, and ran out of the room.

I was kind of reeling from Bailey's answer—I mean, who says no to being shown the ropes? Was she so cool that she didn't need any help, or did she just not want *my* help? Had I stepped in some poop or something? I tried to check my shoes without being too obvious about it, then said, "Yeah, totally, whatever, cool," which was the most meaningless series of words I could string together.

"Here are ze ropes!" Klaus announced, back from wherever he had disappeared to, and threw three giant ropes at Bailey's feet, the kind we climb in gym class. "Look at ze ropes, Bailey! Zere zey are!"

"Nice ropes," said Bailey. "Thanks, Klaus."

"Klaus's pleasure!" said Klaus. He bowed from the waist, scooped up the ropes, and scurried away.

"Told Bailey this place was weird," I said cheerfully, deciding I was being a goober and there was no reason to worry. If Bailey liked to figure stuff out on her own, that was fine. I'd just talk about something else. One thing Jake Liston knows how to do is run his mouth.

"Does Bailey like comedy?" I asked. "Because, you know—I mean, Bailey knows—I mean, wait, no, Jake means . . . that Bailey knows, Jake does stand-up every week at a place downtown called the Yuk-Yuk." Bailey looked confused. I didn't blame her—I couldn't really follow what I'd just said, either. I made a mental note to get food poisoning next Third-Person Thursday.

"Um . . . comedy is cool," Bailey said, and brushed her bangs out of her eyes. But from the tone of her voice, she was just being polite. I could have asked her anything:

Me: Hey, Bailey, wanna take a swim with me in this giant vat of rancid camel throw-up?

Bailey: Swimming is cool.

Me: Bailey, how about I take you out to dinner at this restaurant that serves gluten-free ravioli stuffed with live worms, rotten hamburger meat, and horse snot?

Bailey: Eating is cool.

Clearly, if I was going to make any impression on Bailey whatsoever, I needed to take a different approach. I had no idea what that approach was, but I did know who to ask.

CHAPTER 3

My parents and Pierre's wouldn't let Conceptual Art Band tour, which was a real bummer for Lisa and Pierre since playing shows is pretty much the most fun thing a band gets to do. Also, as Lisa explained to my parents approximately fourteen bajillion times during the You Have to Let Us Tour War, nobody actually buys music anymore, so playing shows and selling merch (which is short for merchandise, but if you're cool you just say merch, though I always imagine merch as some kind of tropical bird, I don't know why) is the only way you can make any real money.

MERCH IN ITS NATURAL HABITAT

My parents and Pierre's were not convinced. So instead, Conceptual Art Band decided to do a Reverse Tour. If you have no idea what that is, don't feel bad, because Pierre and Lisa made it up. Nobody else in the history of music has ever tried it before— probably because it's completely insane. Then again, nobody had ever written a song about a platypus before, either, and look how that turned out.

The concept of the Reverse Tour was that since Pierre and Lisa couldn't travel to play shows for their fans in different cities, their fans in different cities could travel here to see them play at the Yuk-Yuk every Tuesday, Thursday, and Sunday.

That part is not so weird. The weird part is that ONLY people from whatever city they were reverse-touring were allowed in on any given night. If it was Cleveland night, then only people from Cleveland could attend the show. And on Dakar night, don't even think about getting into the club without a Senegalese passport.

It sounds like an idea you might come up with after

falling down and hitting your head, but tonight was the eighth show of the Reverse Tour, and so far every single one had sold out. There hadn't actually been a Dakar night (yet), but Conceptual Art Band had packed the house with residents of New York City, Denver, Durham, Cleveland, Oakland, Barcelona (they did the whole show in Spanish that night), and Tokyo. I assume they chose the cities based on where they thought they had the most fans, but knowing Pierre and Lisa, it just as easily could have been for some other reason, like "only cities whose latitude and longitude add up to prime numbers" or "only cities with zoos that have a camel" or whatever.

Tonight was Stockholm, which was apparently teeming with Conceptual Art Band fans, judging from the line snaking from the door of the Yuk-Yuk all the way to the frozen yogurt place on the corner.

"How's it feel out there, kiddo?" Maury Kovalski asked me when I walked into the green room, which isn't green. It's kind of mauve, with peeling paint and thirty years' worth of spilled drinks soaked into the carpet. But one thing I've learned about show business is that the room you wait in before you go onstage is always called the green room. I asked Maury why once, and he patted me on the cheek and said, "Nobody knows, Salvatore." There was something sticky on his fingers, probably the honey he likes to squeeze into the tubs of yogurt he always seems to be eating.

When I pointed out that my name isn't Salvatore, he said, "Don't get wise with me, Sally Boy." Conversations with Maury can be kind of unpredictable. You might think he was losing his marbles a little bit, but the truth is that Maury Kovalski is as sharp as a tack, even if he is almost five hundred thousand million years old. There's always a reason he says the things he does, even if I can't always figure it out.

In that case, for example, he was calling me Salvatore as a way to cue me to start improvising. I was supposed to take that line, *Nobody knows, Salvatore,* and figure out what it was that nobody knew and say something back that would open up possibilities for the scene— hit the ball into his court so we could start volleying it back and forth like a pair of professional tennis players. For example, a good response would have been: "Then I guess we'll just have to sneak into the sausage factory and see how they do it for ourselves, Aunt Janice."

The reason Maury was waiting for me in the green room, and the reason he said things to me like *Nobody knows, Salvatore*, was that Maury Kovalski and I were now a comedy team. We called ourselves the Old Man and the C Student, which was a play on the title of a famous book by Ernest Hemingway called *The Old Man and the Sea*, which I have not read but I guess it's about some geezer who likes to fish or something.

The Old Man and the C Student was the opening act for Conceptual Art Band. Our routine was different every night, because it was all improvised. We'd have the audience call out ideas for who we were, and we'd have a conversation based on whatever they picked. On Sunday, I was a cop and Maury was a jelly donut. The Thursday before that, he was a talking dolphin and I was LeBron James. (That was the Cleveland show, obviously.)

"It feels good out there," I said. "Warm crowd. Ready to laugh."

"Good," Maury said, and stuffed a forkful of calamari into his mouth. "You know the key to the whole shebang, sonny?"

"You mean the key the wizard keeps on a chain around his neck?" I shot right back, steering him into a *Lord of the Rings*–type thing and thinking maybe we were a couple of bozo Orcs.

Maury waved me off. "I'm not doing a bit, schlemiel. I'm getting ready to teach you something."

"It's definitely not table manners," I said, as Maury dribbled cocktail sauce all over his backstage bathrobe, which was sometimes also his onstage bathrobe.

"The key," he went on, ignoring that, "is *yes, and.* Not just the key to improv. The key to life."

"Yes, and," I repeated.

"Whatever I throw you onstage, and whatever life throws you, the trick is to go with it. You say yes, and then you add on. 'Hey, Dimitri, whaddaya say we jump in the car?' 'Yes, and let's bring the cats with us.' You get it?"

"I think so."

"He thinks so. You know what kills improv? Kills everything? *No. No* leaves you with bupkes. Allow me to demonstrate. 'Hey, Martha Washington, how about you and me redecorate the White House?' 'No.' Bam, stake through the heart. The scene is dead. See what I mean?"

"Yeah. What's bupkes?"

"Bupkes is Yiddish."

"I know that. What's it mean?"

"Bupkes is nada. Zilch. Zero."

"It sounds like butt kiss."

Bupkes is also the surname of legendary football Hall-o'-Famer Dick Bupkes!!

If I were still alive, I'd kick you in the bupkes!!

"Real mature. This is what I get for working with a six-year-old."

"I'm twelve.

"Six, thirteen, same difference. I got boogers older than you."

Yes, and sounded like a pretty good philosophy. I thought about this new baby that was coming and tried to *yes, and* my way into some enthusiasm.

Hey, a new baby! I bet you can't wait to be a big brother!

Yes, and get woken up every night by screams!

Wow, you and the baby will have a lifelong bond! Isn't that cool?

Yes, and that bond will be very similar to the bond between two guys sharing a prison cell, which is what my/our bedroom is going to feel like, except that it will probably smell worse!

Hey, what if the baby is better than you at everything, even comedy? Do you think that could happen?

Yes, and I'm beginning to think that yes, and may not be the best philosophy after all.

Hey, are you talking to yourself out loud in two different voices?

Yes, and that is also probably not the best idea.

"You done, kid?" Maury asked.

"Yeah," I said. "Sorry."

"Were you trying out a bit, or are you really gonna be a big brother?"

"I'm really gonna be a big brother."

"Mazel tov," said Maury. "That means congratulations. Except, wait, it's bad luck to congratulate before the baby is born. I take it back." He shoved a spoonful of yogurt into his mouth, followed by a spoonful of honey.

Just then, Pierre and Lisa walked into the dressing room. "Packed house," Lisa reported. "Man, Swedes are tall."

"I learned some Swedish to open with," Pierre announced, and then for the next thirty seconds or so he spoke Swedish. At least, I assume it was Swedish. It could have been baby talk and I wouldn't know the difference.

"What's it mean?" I asked when he was done.

"Hello," said Pierre. "My friends call me the Admiral. I do not know my way around Stockholm, but I need to find two hundred monkey costumes immediately. Can you help me?"

"Rad," said Lisa, nodding in approval.

"What about you, G.I. Bro?" Pierre asked, sitting next to me on the couch. "Ready to do your thing? Any questions, concerns, or comments?"

"Actually, yeah," I said. "I do kind of need some advice."

"Never water-ski on dry land," said Maury. "Never trust a woman named Sheila the Knucklehead to manage your finances. Don't eat oysters on a—"

"I mean specific advice, about a specific thing," I clarified. "There's this new girl in my class. Bailey."

Lisa smiled and poked me in the arm. "Uh-oh, Jake's got a crush."

"I guess," I said. "I dunno. Maybe. I just want to get to know her, but I can't figure out how."

"Do it in class," said Lisa. "Take it slow. Keep it natural."

I shrugged. "But school is so weird and unpredictable. I can never guess what Mr. Allen's going to make us do next. I mean, tomorrow we start Art and Criticism, and I don't even know if that's one thing or two separate things. Or maybe we're just going to be sitting around insulting some guy named Art."

KeePiNg iT NaTuraL

"I spent a winter that way once," said Maury. "Good times."

"Common interests," said Pierre. "That's the key,

Bro-man Candle. Find out what she likes to do, and do it with her."

"Having stuff in common is important," Lisa agreed. "That's what brought Pierre and me together."

"Music," I said, nodding.

Pierre and Lisa scowled. "Dinosaur reenactment club," they said together.

"But what if Bailey and I don't have any common interests?" I asked.

"Don't be a schnook," said Maury. "Everybody has something in common."

I thought about that for a second. It seemed logical enough.

"Or if not, just pretend you like what she likes," Maury added, and shoved a chicken wing into his mouth.

CHAPTER 4

Sometimes you've got to grab the bull by the horns, as the old expression goes, although the part they forgot to add is *even though you will probably get trampled to death and a way better idea is to just leave the bull alone, or maybe give it a quick high-five and keep on walking.* In this case, the bull was Bailey. Or, no, actually, the bull was talking to Bailey. Me talking to Bailey, that is. Although a bull prob-ably could have done a better job of talking to her than I did.

First thing Friday morning, I marched straight up to her, my head still buzzing with all the advice I'd gotten from Maury, Lisa, and Pierre.

"Hey, Bailey," I said, tapping her on the shoulder. She turned around and said, "Hey, The Dentist," which was a very promising start, since The Dentist was a nickname I'd given myself at the beginning of the school year when I first launched my Outweirdo the Weirdos campaign of trying to fit in by not fitting in. But nobody had called me The Dentist in a while, so Bailey's using it must have meant somebody had told her about it. And *that* must have meant Bailey had been asking questions about me.

"How'd you know my nickname?" I asked, trying not to show how pleased I was.

"Because it's written on your name tag," she said, pointing. Sure enough, I had one of those

HI, MY NAME IS . . . stickers plastered to my shirt, which they'd made us all wear for a class field trip to the reptile park, I guess so they knew who was a mammal and who wasn't.

Now that I thought about it, this also solved the mystery of why I smelled vaguely of iguana. I really should do laundry more often.

"Oh," I said. "Right. So, uh, anyway—you're into hair, right?"

Bailey nodded. "Wig making." She crinkled up her nose. "Do you smell that?"

"Cool," I said, ignoring the question, "because it just so happens that I'm a pretty amazing barber."

Saying that was not part of the plan. The plan was to say something like *Wig making sounds cool. Maybe you could teach me how sometime?* But apparently, aliens who had flown across the galaxy for the sole purpose of humiliating me had seized control of my brain.

Alien #1: Haha, now let's have him invite her over to his "home salon" to watch him give haircuts.

Alien #2: But he doesn't have a home salon! Nobody in their right mind would let him cut their hair!

49

Alien #1: That's why it's funny, dingus!

Alien #2: Ohhhhhh, yeah. Hey, maybe he could also throw up all over her?

Alien #1: Too much.

By the time the bell rang for homeroom, Bailey had accepted my (I mean, the aliens') generous invitation to come over and watch me ply my craft at the ol' home hair salon that afternoon. I don't really remember anything else about school, because I spent the rest of the day

Scissors

Mirror

Clippers

Bandages

wondering exactly how I was going to pull this off. I had scissors and a mirror and I could borrow my dad's electric shaver, so that part wasn't a problem. But there was only one way I was going to have any customers, and that was to call in some big-time favors.

As soon as I got home, I dialed Maury Kovalski. He picked up on the sixteenth ring, which is about standard for him, and said, "Francine's Road Kill Café, you kill 'em, we grill 'em."

"Maury, it's Jake. I need a favor."

"Whaddaya need, a senator blackmailed?"

"Uh . . . no," I said.

I heard him snap his fingers. "You want me to poison a racehorse, don't you? I've been waiting for this call."

"I just want to give you a haircut."

"What makes you think I'd let you cut my hair?"

"Mostly the fact that you don't own a mirror."

Maury thought that over, and then said, "Anything for you, bubbeleh. I could use a trim anyway. It's either that or buy a violin. What do you know about cutting hair, anyway?"

"Nothing. I'm doing it to impress Bailey."

"Thattaboy. Never be afraid to make a fool of yourself."

That didn't seem like the most inspiring advice, but I'd take what I could get. A butt in the barber's chair was a butt in the barber's chair.

"Right on," I said weakly.

"Send a car," said Maury. "A car with oatmeal in it. Brown sugar, raisins, a little bit of cream. Not that instant stuff, either. Steel-cut oats. Organic." And with that, he hung up.

I was pretty sure I could convince Pierre to chauffeur Maury, because although he was currently rehearsing in the attic with Lisa, he basically looked for any excuse to drive the Porsche he bought when "The Ballad of the Duck-Billed Platypus" blew up. As for the oatmeal, I could make it. We didn't have raisins, but we did have dried cranberries, which I was guessing would blow Maury's mind.

First, though, I had to line up another customer. And that wasn't going to be easy.

I walked down the block to my best friend Evan's house. He was shooting hoops in his driveway.

"Hey, dude," he said, bounce-passing me the ball. "Wanna play HORSE?"

"I do," I said. "But I can't. I came to ask you for a favor." I attempted a hook shot, and the ball hit the side of the backboard and ricocheted into Mrs. Murphy's yard next door.

"Basketball lessons?" Evan asked.

"Your mother needs basketball lessons."

"No, she doesn't. My mother played Division One college ball."

"Oh, yeah," I said. "Maybe she could give *me* basketball lessons."

"I'm sure she'd love to. You're like a son to her. Want me to ask right now? Hey, Mom!" Evan called.

This was getting out of hand. "No, dude," I said. "I was just trying to insult

you back. I forgot your mom was a successful college athlete. Can I ask you this favor, or what?"

"Go for it, The Dentist. Also, do you know you smell like iguana?"

"Yes, I'm aware. Okay, so here it is: I need you to help me pretend to be a barber to impress this girl Bailey."

"Sure," said Evan, rubbing his hands together with glee. He loved a good caper. "How about this: I put on a fake mustache from my junior detective kit, and then I just accidentally 'happen' to run into you and Bailey, and in a French accent, I say, 'Ah, oui, sacré bleu! I do

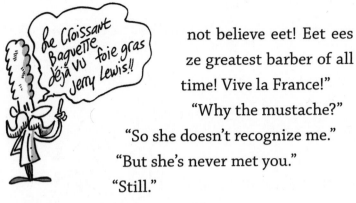

le Croissant
Baguette
déjà vu foie gras
Jerry Lewis!!

not believe eet! Eet ees ze greatest barber of all time! Vive la France!"

"Why the mustache?"

"So she doesn't recognize me."

"But she's never met you."

"Still."

"And why the French accent?"

"To make the whole thing seem more authentic."

"And why 'vive la France'?"

"Because French people are always saying that."

"It's a good plan," I said. "But I need you to let me cut your hair."

Evan covered his hair with both hands. "What? Never!"

"Come on, man. I'll do a good job. Name your price."

Evan thought about it for a minute, then said, "You can't put a price on self-esteem."

"Try."

"You gotta buy me dinner," Evan decided.

"Done." We shook hands, and I breathed a huge sigh of relief. "Thanks for letting me off easy."

"We'll see about that," Evan said ominously, and right on cue a big dark cloud floated across the face of the sun and cast us both into shadow. "Now, what's this I hear about a new baby?"

"How'd you know about that?"

"I saw it on CNN," said Evan. "What do you think, schlemiel? Your mom called my mom."

"Oh."

"You don't seem very excited about it."

Evan is my best friend, so I wasn't about to pretend with him. "I'm not," I said.

"I don't blame you. Your parents are way too old for a baby. You know who's gonna end up raising that little crumb snatcher? You, that's who. I've seen it a million times."

"Where have you seen it a million times?"

"Well, maybe not a million. Maybe like twice. Once in this movie, I forget what it's called, but this ten-year-old is basically like his baby sister's servant. It's horrifying."

"And the other time?"

"Huh?"

"You said you'd seen it twice."

"Oh." Evan scratched his head. "I guess I

watched that movie a couple of times. But still. I mean, jeez—quit while you're ahead. First, your parents had an awesome kid. Then they had a decent one. Each kid is getting worse. What if this one is a monster?"

"Thanks," I said. "I feel so much better now. I'm really ready to focus on cutting hair."

• • •

An hour later, I had Maury seated in my makeshift barber chair, with an old Star Wars bedsheet tied around his neck.

Evan sat in a beanbag chair, waiting his turn.

Although, actually, all of us were waiting for Bailey. Maury had been sitting like that for twenty minutes already. He'd been telling us old jokes the whole time, which was definitely helping to keep me loose.

"So I went to the doctor," he was saying now. "I told him I broke my leg in two places, and you know what he said?"

Evan shrugged. I looked down at the scissors in my hand for the millionth time, strategizing

about what I was going to do to Maury's full head of fluffy white hair.

"Stop going to those places," Maury finished. That was when the doorbell rang.

I ran upstairs and opened it, and there was Bailey.

"Come on in," I said. "I was just about to get started. Right this way."

CHAPTER 5

I led Bailey into the salon and introduced her to Maury and Evan.

"Howdy, kiddo," said Maury, waving his hand underneath the sheet.

"Howdy to you, too," she said back.

"I'm Evan," said Evan.

"I know," said Bailey. "The Dentist just said that."

"Oh, right," said Evan. "You here for a haircut?"

"No," said Bailey. "Just for some hair." She pulled a giant plastic bag out of her backpack, then looked at me and added, "That's okay, right?"

"Sure, sure," I said. "Now, what'll it be today, Maury? The usual?"

"Make it the unusual," said Maury. "You only live once."

"You got it," I said, and started cutting. Bailey and Evan chatted, but I couldn't focus on what they were saying because I was busy concentrating on Maury. The lucky thing was that he had a lot of hair, so I just kind of snipped at the edges for a while and tried to keep both sides even. When I'd been at it for about ten minutes, I decided to quit while I was ahead, so I tapped him on the shoulder and said, "How's that?"

Maury, who had been asleep since the first snip, startled awake and said, "Incredible!" And he was right: it was pretty incredible, in that he looked basically the same as when he'd sat down. I untied the sheet, feeling pleased with myself, and waited while Bailey swept all the hair into her bag.

"You're up," I told Evan. He shot me a secret look of

screw this up and I will make you pay, and then he let me tie the sheet around his neck. Bailey took out a second bag.

"Just a trim," Evan said, staring daggers at me.

"No sweat, Chet," I said cheerfully. Then I realized the problem. Evan's hair was already pretty short. To get it any shorter, I was going to have to use the clippers. Scissors, they teach you how to use in kindergarten. Clippers, not so much. I knew more about the Los Angeles Clippers than I did about the ones I was holding.

THE CLIPPERS HAVE TRADITIONALLY BEEN A POOR PERFORMING BASKETBALL TEAM...

BUT we look good!!

"Okay," I said, "here we go." I set the clippers on their lowest setting, which was conveniently labeled "1," figuring I'd just kind of graze the top of Evan's head.

Looking back, it seems obvious that "1" and "lowest setting" could mean multiple things. Like, for example, the lowest setting might be the one that left the least hair, or even no hair at all. That did not occur to me until about two seconds after I pressed the clippers to the middle of the top of my best friend's head and started to clip.

I guess you would call what happened a Reverse Mohawk. Or maybe a Landing Strip in the Forest. When I saw what I'd done, I almost dropped the clippers in horror.

"What?" said Evan, hearing me gasp.

"Nothing," I said, smiling at Bailey. "Same cut as always, Bro-ba Fett. Relax and let me work my magic."

Magic was definitely what I needed. I switched the clippers to "5," figuring that if I made the rest of his hair shorter, the landing strip would be less noticeable.

Then I kind of faded the sides up, and tried to blend everything together. By the time I finished, I was sweating so hard I could barely grip the clippers, which is probably why they slipped and sliced a cool little line through Evan's left eyebrow.

"Okay," I said at last. "Done."

Evan brought his hands up to his head and felt around.

"Mirror," he said. "Now."

I handed it to him.

Evan's eyes got wide, and his face turned crimson.

"I'm going to kill—"

"Dude . . . ," I hissed, low enough that Bailey didn't hear.

"—my . . . last barber, because . . . he's . . . not the . . . genius you are!" Evan finished, all the while staring at me like he was imagining pulling my lower intestines out of my body and jumping rope with them.

"Another satisfied customer," I said, smiling at Bailey.

"Pretty rad, huh?" Evan said, turning to model his haircut for her. I had to give him credit: this was a total, 100 percent dumpster fire, and he was acting his butt off like a champ.

"Um, yeah, I guess," said Bailey, scooping the last of his fallen hair into her bag. "Well, thanks for the hair, Jake. I should probably be going."

"We were gonna grab some dinner," I said. "Do you want to join us?"

"Thanks, but I gotta boogie. See you in school tomorrow. Nice to meet you guys."

Before I could respond, Bailey was gone. I couldn't tell if she'd even been impressed. I was used to kids at M&AA being pretty over the top; if somebody was happy or sad or angry or embarrassed, you could usually tell from fifty feet away. But Bailey was different. I couldn't figure out what made her tick or how she thought. Somehow that made me like her even more.

● ● ●

As it turned out, it was a good thing Bailey bailed on dinner, because it was one of the most disgusting things I've ever been a part of. Evan decided to make me pay for what I'd done to his hair by buying him as much food as he could possibly consume. I guess he never heard the expression that revenge is a dish best served cold.

First, we went to Paulie's Pizza. They have four sizes, from small to extra-large. An extra-large is what my whole family orders to share. Evan marched up to the counter, where Paulie Jr. was standing, and said, "Little Paulie, let me ask you a question: what's your most expensive pizza?"

Little Paulie (who weighs about twice what his dad, Big Paulie, weighs) turned and squinted up at the menu on the wall. "The Hawaiian, I guess," he said.

"Is there a way to make it *more* expensive?" Evan asked.

"Uh . . . you could add some extra toppings, but then it ain't really a Hawaiian no more."

"Great," said Evan. "Give me an extra-large, with all the toppings."

Little Paulie's jaw dropped. "All of them?"

"Every single one." Evan jerked his thumb at me. "And whatever this schlemiel is having."

For the next hour, I sat in silence and watched Evan systematically destroy the biggest, heaviest, grossest pizza I'd ever seen. Little Paulie and the guys in the kitchen came out to watch after a while, and I saw them muttering to each other and passing money back and forth. I'm pretty sure they were betting on how much he could eat. If they'd asked me, I could have told them: never bet against Evan's stomach, and never bet against Evan if he's angry.

When he ate the last bite of the last slice, the whole restaurant burst into applause.

Evan patted his stomach and said, "I'm ready for dessert now, Mr. Barber Man."

"Sure," I said wearily, and followed him next door to the ice cream place.

"Oink," said Evan to the girl behind the counter. That was how you ordered the famous Tub for Two, a concoction that the sign on the wall described like this:

A boatload of chocolate sauce, a lake of caramel, a hailstorm of chopped nuts, six scoops of ice cream, a cloud of whipped cream, nineteen cherries, four crushed-up cookies, twelve marshmallows, and a banana. (If you get full, you can always skip the banana.)

appropriate "spoon"

strenuous pre-ice cream warm-ups

Evan didn't skip the banana.

"Sorry about the haircut," I said when he was finished.

"Eh," said Evan, "I knew what I was getting into. Whatever. It will grow back."

"So you're not mad anymore?"

"I'm too full to be mad," said Evan. Then he let out a burp so loud it probably disrupted radio transmissions across three counties.

CHAPTER 6

The next day, Mr. Allen gave us our first Art and Criticism assignment: to write and shoot the worst film we could.

"Why?" asked Zenobia.

"Right on," said Mr. Allen, nodding.

"What if we make a good film by accident?" asked Azure, which makes sense because she is basically incapable of doing anything badly.

"Just do the best you can," said Mr. Allen.

"You mean the *worst* we can," said Forrest.

"Do your best to make it bad," Mr. Allen clarified, unclarifyingly.

"Can we do our worst to make it good?" asked Bin-Bin.

I'm a STAH!!

ze WURST film?

KLAUS WAS even MORE CONFUSED.

"Absolutely not," said Mr. Allen firmly.

"How do we know what's bad?" I asked.

"Ah-ha!" Mr. Allen walked over and gave me a high five. "The Dentist is on to something here."

We all waited for him to continue, but instead he wandered away and started cleaning Hotch's cage.

There was a whole fifty-seven minutes left before lunch, so everybody opened their notebooks and started writing. It was an interesting idea, once you got over the weirdness of it. What made a bad movie bad? I jotted down some notes.

Badness

- Make sure boom microphone is in every single shot.
- Get worst actors possible, then do not let them rehearse.
- Make sure camerawork is really bad (shaky, out of focus, pointing in wrong direction).
- Or maybe forget to remove lens cap from camera altogether and shoot the whole movie in pitch-black.
- What is the movie about? Nobody knows. Dialogue is just random words, like one person

says, "Pineapple diagram malodorous tricer-
atops pantaloons," and another person says,
"Sunscreen tracksuit henchman silly monocle."

- The entire cast is babies, and none of the babies
  are cute, funny, or interesting. None of them
  can even fart at the right time.

At first, I was really excited about how truly terrible my movie sounded. But then I stopped and thought
about the difference between *bad* and *incompetent
and nonsensical.* Most of what I was describing was
either incompetent (the boom mic in every shot) or
nonsensical (the dialogue). Maybe bad was harder than
that. Anybody could dangle boom mics and make shots
fuzzy. But that would be taking the easy way.

I crossed out everything I had written, then
thought about what a movie *was.* It was a story. So
you couldn't just make a movie that didn't have a
story—that would be bad, but it wouldn't be a movie.

What you needed was a story that was both dumb and totally unoriginal. You needed characters so flat they seemed like they were made out of cardboard.

WANTED: CHARACTER FLATTER THAN 3-DAY-OLD SODA

A plot that made no sense, not because it was supposed to be absurd but because it was full of more holes than my dad's lucky college socks. Basically a movie that insulted the intelligence of everyone who saw it, even morons.

THE ONLY THINGS HOLIER THAN JAKE'S PLOT:

GOOD eatin'!!

A PIECE OF SWISS CHEESE!!

A MOTH-RIDDEN GYM SOCK!!

Then it hit me that I was describing practically every big Hollywood blockbuster I'd ever seen, and all I had to do was write a movie exactly like the ones that made five hundred million dollars every summer, only much shorter. It turned out to be surprisingly easy.

ACTION HERO SAVES THE WORLD
By "Clippers" Liston

FADE IN on ACTION HERO. He is a dude in his late thirties who looks vaguely familiar, like maybe he has been in a bunch of successful action movies. But also he would be semi-believable as a strangely muscular lawyer.

Action Hero is lying on a towel in a bathing suit. The towel is lying on a yacht. The yacht speeds through the water.

Action Hero stands up and speaks to his friend JIMMY, who is a regular-looking guy in a Hawaiian shirt.

ACTION HERO: Something doesn't feel right, Jimmy.

JIMMY: Well, it couldn't be Count Von Candybar, because you killed him. You killed him dead.

Action Hero grimaces in a compelling manner.

ACTION HERO: Mmmh.

All of a sudden, Action Hero ducks and looks over the side of the yacht.

Four HENCHMEN in the latest nautical hench-wear are riding on the backs of dolphins.

HENCHMAN: Count Von Candybar sends his greetings!

A volley of flaming spears tears through the side of the yacht, and it EXPLODES INTO FLAMES.

Just in the nick of time, Action Hero jumps off the yacht and onto the back of one of the dolphins. He repeatedly punches the henchman riding the dolphin, until he falls off the dolphin.

Out of nowhere, a HUMONGOUS SHARK surfaces and eats the henchman.

Grimly, to himself, Action Hero says:

ACTION HERO: Better brush your teeth after a meal like that.

But then all three remaining henchmen start shooting flaming spears at him! Action Hero's dolphin is hit. Angrily, Action Hero shouts:

ACTION HERO: Wrong kind of blowhole!

He has no choice: Action Hero jumps onto the back of the shark, who is trying to swallow the henchman's spear. He grabs a rope and uses it to make one of those things you put on a horse, a bit or whatever. Now Action Hero can control the shark!

ACTION HERO: Jump, boy, jump!

Somehow the shark is obeying his every command. He jumps high into the air, and Action Hero takes three throwing stars out of the pockets of his bathing suit and throws them at the henchmen. All three henchmen fall off their dolphins, and the water bubbles.

Action Hero has a grim look on his face as he surveys the devastation.

ACTION HERO: Now take me home.

The shark turns around and swims toward home.

INTERIOR—ACTION HERO'S BOSS'S OFFICE

It's an all-glass room in a skyscraper. Action Hero's

boss paces angrily behind her desk. Action Hero slouches in a chair, looking grim but also bored.

Behind him, on the couch, lies the shark. The shark is now Action Hero's best friend. He wears a HIGH-TECH BREATHING APPARATUS invented by a GOVERNMENT SCIENTIST who is also a SUPERMODEL.

BOSS: That's it, Action Hero. I've had just about enough of your reckless, heroic behavior, followed by amusing wisecracks. And also your grim looks. And Count Von Candybar is definitely dead.

ACTION HERO: If he's so dead, how come he tried to kill me?

BOSS: Enough of your insubordination. You're suspended.

ACTION HERO: (to the shark) You hear that, Jimmy? I'm suspended. Boo hoo.

BOSS: That's it! Both of you, out of my office!

ACTION HERO: You ain't gotta tell me twice. Come on, Jimmy. Let's go fight some crime.

INTERIOR—THE UNDERGROUND LAIR OF COUNT VON CANDYBAR

Twenty COMPUTER GUYS sit at their terminals looking busy and worried. The evil COUNT VON CANDYBAR walks around the perimeter, speaking to his top aide and personal biographer, VANESSA.

COUNT VON CANDYBAR: As you know, Vanessa, I am not really dead. I faked my death.

VANESSA: Yes, sir. I remember.

COUNT VON CANDYBAR: And now that Action Hero is dead, my complicated plan to take over the global petroleum market *using computers* [he gestures to all the computers] can finally happen!

A computer guy raises his hand.

COMPUTER GUY: Sir? Action Hero is not dead. It seems he escaped.

FUN (FAKE) FACTS about... PETROLEUM!

"PETROLEUM" IS THE go-TO word for POETS WHEN looking for a word THAT rHymes WITH "LINOLEUM"!!

PETROLEUM jelly IS THE THIRD MOST POPULAR SPREAD ON TOAST IN WINNEEGEECHEE, MANITOBA!! (BEHIND PLUM & STRAWBERRY!!)

PETROLEE-YUM!

Count Von Candybar walks over to the guy, enraged.

COUNT VON CANDYBAR: How is this possible?

COMPUTER GUY: I mean, I was sitting right here, so I'm not totally sure, but—

COUNT VON CANDYBAR: I'm sick of your excuses!

He pulls out a remote control and presses a button. A trapdoor opens underneath Computer Guy, and he falls screaming into a pit full of SNAKES.

COUNT VON CANDYBAR: I want Action Hero dead!

EXTERIOR—A CAFÉ IN PARIS—DAY

Action Hero and Jimmy the Shark are sitting at a table with a couple of cappuccinos in front of them.

ACTION HERO: According to that nerd I was telling you about, Count Von Candybar is either in Monaco, Moscow, or Minnesota. Someplace that starts with an M.

He picks up his cappuccino—and it explodes!

ACTION HERO: JIMMY! GET DOWN!

Flaming spears start flying everywhere. Fifteen spearmen jump on motorcycles and peel off. Action Hero knocks one off his bike and grabs his flaming spear.

For the next fifteen minutes, he chases them around the alleys and streets of Paris, causing the destruction of twenty-nine outdoor fruit stands. They also do a bunch of stuff nobody has ever done on motorcycles before, like balance on railings, jump from one skyscraper to another, balance on the backs of horses, etc. Very thrilling stuff.

Eventually, the LAST GUY gets away by jumping his bike onto an ocean liner. But Action Hero finds a COMPUTER DRIVE on the ground. He picks it up and scowls grimly at it.

ACTION HERO: Bingo.

He folds his fist around it.

ACTION HERO: This one's for Jimmy.

INTERIOR—THE OVERGROUND PART OF THE UNDERGROUND LAIR OF COUNT VON CANDYBAR—EVENING

Count Von Candybar and Vanessa are drinking wine. He's wearing a tuxedo, and she's wearing an evening gown.

COUNT VON CANDYBAR: So then, you understand my plan to *use computers* to take over the whole world?

VANESSA: Yes. It's brilliant, Count Von Candybar.

He takes a sip of wine.

COUNT VON CANDYBAR: This wine cost one million dollars.

He picks up a carrot stick and dips it in hummus.

COUNT VON CANDYBAR: And this hummus cost two million dollars.

VANESSA: Wow. You have to give me the recipe.

COUNT VON CANDYBAR: Of course.

He claps his hands and in comes CHEF ELIHU.

COUNT VON CANDYBAR: Chef Elihu, give Miss Vanessa the hummus recipe.

ELIHU: Ah, oui. In a food processor, combine garlic, garbanzo beans, tahini, lemon juice, a half cup water, and olive oil. Process until smooth. Add salt, starting at half a teaspoon, to taste. Spoon into a serving dish, swirl a little olive oil over the top, and sprinkle with toasted pine nuts and chopped parsley.

FUN (Fake) FACTS about: HUMMUS!!

Hummmmmm

Perfectly made Hummus makes a **Humming Noise** when you place the container to your ear!!

How to react to great-tasting Hummus:

Yum!! ←NO

Hum!! Yes!!

VANESSA: Oh, that's pretty easy.

COUNT VON CANDYBAR: Thank you, Chef Elihu.

He takes out a remote control and presses a button. A trapdoor opens underneath Chef Elihu, and he plummets, screaming, into a PIT FULL OF BEAVERS.

Count Von Candybar smiles at Vanessa.

COUNT VON CANDYBAR: And now it is all yours.

Just then, Action Hero SWINGS THROUGH THE STAINED-GLASS WINDOW ON A ROPE. As he enters, he yells:

ACTION HERO: Now I'm gettin' into the swing of it!

Count Von Candybar takes out his remote control. Action Hero lands atop a trapdoor, which opens. He falls into a PIT FULL OF KOMODO DRAGONS.

Count Von Candybar peers down at him.

COUNT VON CANDYBAR: Thanks for dropping in.

Action Hero looks up grimly. Then he grimaces.

ACTION HERO: Vanessa?

VANESSA: Action Hero?

COUNT VON CANDYBAR: You two know each other?

VANESSA: He's my ex-husband.

ACTION HERO: I haven't signed those divorce papers yet.

A KOMODO DRAGON hisses at him, and he punches it in the face. Then another, and another.

COUNT VON CANDYBAR: Goodbye, Action Hero.

He closes the panel over the trapdoor, sealing Action Hero inside.

COUNT VON CANDYBAR: Now, for the final step in my plan to become the unchallenged Master of the Universe, *using computers*.

He picks up a walkie-talkie.

COUNT VON CANDYBAR: Execute the protocols.

The voice of a computer guy responds.

COMPUTER GUY: Executing the protocols.

Suddenly, there's a crashing sound, and Count Von Candybar turns to see Action Hero's fist SMASHING THROUGH THE FLOOR.

ACTION HERO: Did somebody say *execute*?

He climbs through the floor and THROWS A KOMODO DRAGON at Count Von Candybar. They struggle for a while, until Action Hero finger-whistles. The Komodo dragon looks at him, awaiting orders.

ACTION HERO: Back off. This is my fight.

The Komodo dragon respectfully backs away, and Action Hero roundhouse-kicks Count Von Candybar. They fight for a solid fifteen minutes, using all kinds of martial arts techniques and also breaking valuable pieces of art over each other's heads.

Finally, Action Hero kicks Count Von Candybar down into the Komodo dragon pit and says:

ACTION HERO: Now that's the pits.

Vanessa laughs. Action Hero turns to her.

ACTION HERO: Still want that divorce?

VANESSA: Not on your life.

ACTION HERO: Good.

They kiss. It's extra romantic, even with the sounds of forty Komodo dragons tearing Count Von Candybar limb from limb in the background.

VANESSA: Maybe you're wondering why I was working for the evil Count Von Candybar. . . .

ACTION HERO: You can tell me later. Let's beat it.

There's a noise outside the window. Action Hero looks down, and waiting in the ocean is Jimmy.

ACTION HERO: Jimmy! You're alive!

Vanessa takes his hand, and they jump out the window and land on Jimmy's back.

VANESSA: This turned out to be the best Christmas ever.

Action Hero gives her a look that is somehow both grim and happy.

ACTION HERO: Just wait until New Year's.

THE END . . . UNTIL THE SEQUEL(S)

CHAPTER 7

Only after I finished writing my movie did I remember that we were supposed to shoot them. I wasn't quite sure how I was going to do that, since my film basically had no scenes that didn't involve explosions, motorcycle chases, or large aquatic animals. But luckily for me, when I got to school the next morning, Mr. Allen announced a change of plans.

"The twelfth grade is using all the video cameras," he said. "So we will be shooting our movies with our minds."

"Like, imagining them?" asked Bin-Bin.

"Klaus imagines Academy Award for Best Original Screenplay!" shouted Klaus.

"Yes," said Mr. Allen, which was probably the first time he'd

De Oscars look fancier on de Tee Vee!!

answered a question directly all month. "Now. Is every-one ready for the field trip?"

"What field trip?" we all said together.

"To the Museum of Modern Art," said Mr. Allen. At which point the classroom door opened and in walked his buddy Stan the Man with the Van and the Plan, who is pretty much our official class driver.

"Howdy, class," said Stan the Man with the Van and the Plan.

Whitman raised his hand, which was unusual since Whitman pretty much never speaks. He and Stan have a special connection, though, because Whitman really wants a van.

"Yessir, Whitman," said Stan.

"How's your plan?" he asked breathlessly.

"My plan to get another van?"

Whitman nodded eagerly. He seemed to be sweating.

"My plan ran into a toucan clan," said Stan sadly. "The second van ran, but man—they need a toucan ban from Spokane to Japan."

Nobody said anything for a minute. Then Azure said, "So . . . what you're saying is . . . you hit a bird?"

Stan shook his head. "I swerved the van."

"Oh. Good."

"And hit a catamaran. Who's ready to see a Cézanne?"

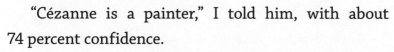

"A what?" asked Forrest.

"Cézanne is a painter," I told him, with about 74 percent confidence.

"No Cézanne today," said Mr. Allen. "Marcel Duchamp. Andy Warhol. We're going to be talking about the concept of the ready-made, and the idea of appropriation."

"It's about time," I said, as if I had any idea what that meant. Everybody laughed.

It turned out to be pretty interesting, actually. Like practically everything Mr. Allen teaches us, it boiled down to the question of what art is. Marcel Duchamp

BAD ARTISTS COPY

GOOD ARTISTS STEAL

EXCEPTIONAL ARTISTS SIP CARBONATED FRUIT COCKTAIL THROUGH A METAL STRAW!!

was this French guy who did stuff like sign his name on a urinal and put it in a museum. He called his pieces "ready-mades," and his point was that anything can be art if you call it art. Or if you look at it a certain way. Or slap your signature on it. Then he stopped making art and just played chess for the last twenty years of his life.

Andy Warhol, meanwhile, was an American dude who is best known for making silkscreens of Campbell's Tomato Soup cans, which was his way of mixing up art and the everyday, and also showing how you could "appropriate" (meaning claim, or steal) stuff and turn it into art. Or maybe he was just really hungry.

Our class was pretty divided over these ideas.

"How is signing your name on a shovel art?"

FUN FAKE FACTS about ANDY WARHOL!!

To Protest WAR, the Pop ARTeest Briefly changed His name to ANDY PEACE-HOL!!

Not a wig!! A ferret!!

His Nickname, "OL' WARY HAND," is an anagram of "ANDY WARHOL"

demanded Zenobia. "I have a Sharpie in my bag. What if I just add my name under his name? Am I a great artist now, too?"

"No, because you didn't think of it," said Azure. "You have to be the first one to think of it."

"Fine, so if I sign my name to, I dunno, a Starbucks cup, then I deserve to be in a museum?"

"The baristas already sign them when you place your order," I pointed out.

"Shut up, Jake," Azure and Zenobia said together.

I walked off and stood with Klaus and Bailey. We stared at one of the Warhol soup cans.

"Zoup," Klaus said after a while. "Vy zoup?"

"Because it was the most boring, everyday, middle-of-the-road thing he could think of," I said. "He

probably grew up eating it, and staring at that label. It probably meant everything and nothing to him at the same time."

Bailey turned to me. "That's really smart," she said, sounding a little surprised.

"I have my moments," I told her. I would have loved to keep going, the deep insights about modern art just flowing out of me, but my moment was over.

The three of us stared awhile longer.

"Zoup," Klaus said again, and I heard his stomach rumble. Maybe it was my imagination, but it seemed to have a German accent.

● ● ●

After school, Mom and Dad took me and Lisa to Baby World, which according to the sign was "Your One-Stop Baby Super Store for

All Your Baby Needs." That seemed like a few more words than necessary, but they probably hadn't paid by the letter, so whatever.

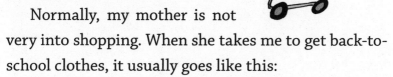

Normally, my mother is not very into shopping. When she takes me to get back-to-school clothes, it usually goes like this:

Mom: T-shirts. You need T-shirts?

Me: Yeah, I guess.

Mom (looking me up and down): What are you, a medium?

Me: There's a fitting room right there. Maybe I—

Mom: I bet you're a medium. (picks up four colors in medium and walks toward the checkout)

But today, she was like a kid in a candy store, or a rocking-chair enthusiast in a rocking-chair store. Or a lover of bacon at a Big Moe's All-You-Can-Eat Bacon Emporium, which is a store that should exist if it does not.

"Oh," she said, stopping suddenly in the middle of an aisle and causing me, Lisa, and my dad, who were following her around like zombies, to rear-end each other. "Look at these. Aren't they darling?"

"What are they?" Lisa asked.

"Spit-up cloths with little bumblebees on them. So cute!" She threw like four hundred of them into the shopping cart.

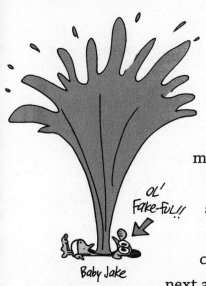

Ol' Fake-ful!!

Baby Jake

"Spit-up cloths?" I repeated. "Like, for puke?"

"Babies puke a lot," my dad said. "You, especially. Oh, man, could you puke."

"I used to call you Pukeymon," said Lisa.

"Oh, and here—a diaper caddy," my mom called from the next aisle over. "That's a must."

"Do I even want to know what that is?" I asked Lisa, feeling a little queasy.

"You fill it with dirty diapers, so they don't stink up your whole house," she answered.

"Gross," I said, imagining a mountain of diapers the size of our house.

She elbowed me in the ribs. "You'll find out all about

THIS IS WHAT I THOUGHT A DIAPER CADDY DID:

Whaddaya think?

Definitely a wedge!!

it when you start changing diapers, Pukeymon."

PUKEYMON GO!! IS A VERY POPULAR CELLPHONE APP THAT SENDS PLAYERS ON A QUEST FOR PUDDLES OF E-PUKE!

FOUND ONE!!

My mother was already at the end of the aisle. "Earplugs," she announced cheerfully. "You kids are gonna need these, especially if the baby has lungs like Lisa."

"Can't . . . wait!" I said gamely. "Sure is gonna be . . . fun!"

We left with two full shopping carts' worth of baby stuff—everything from gates for the stairs to baby butt wipes to books with terrifying titles like *Why Are You Crying, Baby?* and boring titles like *Dog Is Red. Cat Is Blue.* None of it made me feel any better about the whole little-sibling thing. On the contrary, I felt like we were laying in provisions for a long siege by an unreasonable, boring, highly volatile, waste-producing little gremlin.

Luckily, it was a Reverse Tour night at the Yuk-Yuk, so I could blow off some steam with Maury Kovalski in front of two hundred residents of Monmouth, New Hampshire.

I got there early, in time to watch the room fill up and share some green-room mozzarella sticks with Pierre. He asked me how my barbershop move had worked.

"I'm not sure," I said. "She gave me a compliment today, but I haven't really made any headway in, like, getting to know her."

Pierre shook a mozzarella stick at me. "Here's your answer, Walter Bronkite."

"Mozzarella sticks?"

"Food. There's nothing better than cooking somebody a delicious dinner."

I mulled that, imagining me and Bailey sitting down at a quiet table, laughing and talking over a succulent meal. It was a great idea.

I walked onstage full of energy and optimism, ready for whatever the crowd threw at us. You never knew what you were going to get with the Old Man and the C Student, and tonight was no exception. We asked the crowd to give us a question they desperately wanted answered. Usually, everybody shouts at once and you can kind

of cherry-pick the best response. But this time, a lumberjack-looking dude at a front table shouted, *"Can bats swim?"* at the top of his lungs, and we had to go with that, even though it didn't really seem like the most promising premise, at least to me.

This is why Maury is incredible, though. Before I could even wonder how to play it, he started right in:

Maury: Welcome to the first annual Bat Olympics. And here with me, all the way from Baton Rouge, is Mr. Batholomew Batoway. Are you ready for your first event, Mr. Batoway?

Me: It's pronounced Baht-o-way.

Maury: Bahtoway, yes, of course. Are you ready for the 200-meter freestyle, Mr. Bahtoway?

Me: As ready as I'll ever be, I guess.

Maury: How have you prepared for the race?

Me: Well, I've done a bunch of research.

Maury: Research? On what, Mr. Bahtoway?

Me: On whether bats can swim.

Maury: And what have you learned?

Me: Nobody seems to know for sure. Some people say we can float, you know, with the wings and all. Other people are pretty sure we'll drown. But there's only one way to find out, right?

Maury: Yes, by competing in the 200-meter freestyle. Though of course we all remember what happened last year, in the Giraffe Olympics.

Me: Yes, yes, that was tragic. Turns out they can't swim at all. I lost my cousin in that race. He sank right to the bottom. You'd think they could have at least used a regular pool, not a fifty-foot-deep one.

Maury: Your cousin is a giraffe, Mr. Bahtoway?

Me: Well, he *was*.

Maury: What will you do if you win today, Mr. Bahtoway?

Me: I'll probably try the butterfly.

Maury: You'll swim the butterfly?

Me: No, I'll *try* the butterfly. I like it medium rare.

CHAPTER 8

I marched into school the next day determined to take Pierre's advice and invite Bailey over for a home-cooked meal. So as not to make it weird, though, I figured I would invite a few other kids, too—make it a dinner party. But I'd be sure to sit next to her and dazzle her all night with my wit and charm.

The fact that it was Monster Friday made this slightly more difficult. On Monster Friday—as I found out when I walked into the classroom and Mr. Allen presented me with a hat filled with little slips of paper—you had to speak like whatever monster you were assigned.

UNSCRAMBLE THE MOVIE MONSTERS!!

GNLK GNOK _ _ _ _ _ _ _ _

CAARLDU _ _ _ _ _ _ _

HEI MYUMM _ _ _ _ _ _ _ _

LOADGZLL _ _ _ _ _ _ _ _

BIGFOOT!!

THE BRIDE OF FRANKENSTEIN

SWAMP THING (NO NEED for costume!!)

I got Bigfoot, which all in all was a score—compared to, say, Bin-Bin, who got the Mummy and could only make creepy moaning sounds, or Forrest, who got Godzilla and didn't know who Godzilla was because he grew up without a TV and was just walking around saying "I'm Godzilla" in his normal voice. You could even argue that Bigfoot is not a monster at all, just a missing link in evolution who wants to be left alone to pick berries and groom his fellow Bigfoots up there in the forests of the Pacific Northwest. I have a lot of sympathy for Bigfoot, actually. I think we could be friends.

As for how he spoke, I figured he was somewhere between a gorilla and a caveman, so I walked up to Bailey and said, "Bigfoot hosting dinner party tomorrow night. Bigfoot would love if you could attend, although Bigfoot a bit confused as to who you are."

Bailey nodded and made a loud squawking sound, like a pterodactyl with its wing caught in a door. I had no idea who she was supposed to be, but a yes was a yes. There was no reason to keep talking, but as I might have mentioned, I'm not always great at shutting up.

"You are in for treat. Bigfoot five-star gourmet chef. Is no big deal for Bigfoot to make seven-course tasting menu for friends. All top culinary schools want Bigfoot to attend, but Bigfoot say no, too busy slapping grizzly bear in face and showing salmon who is boss."

Bailey squawked again, a little quieter this time, and kind of narrowed her eyes at me like maybe she suspected, correctly, that I was full of baloney. I waved goodbye and moved on. By the end of homeroom, I'd invited everybody. Azure, Forrest, Klaus, and Bailey were sure they could come, Bin-Bin and Zenobia were maybes, and the rest of the class had other plans.

I decided not to panic. I knew how to read. The internet had recipes on it. How hard could it be to whip up a seven-course tasting menu?

• • •

That night, I spent two hours on different cooking websites, planning my menu. I went for stuff that sounded both impressive and delicious.

FIRST COURSE:
miniature spanakopita

SECOND COURSE: cream of cauliflower soup

THIRD COURSE: massaged kale salad with apples and Marcona almonds

FOURTH COURSE: roasted wild salmon with sea beans and oysters

FIFTH COURSE: grapefruit granita

SIXTH COURSE: beef tenderloin with gooseberry sauce

SEVENTH COURSE: apple pie and homemade bacon ice cream

The next day, I took all the money I'd made doing the Old Man and the C Student shows and blew it at the fancy supermarket, on a list of ingredients longer than

FIND THE INGREDIENTS!!

T	Y	W	Y	H	T	C	C	S	P	A	P
S	H	B	U	Q	A	M	I	N	T	B	A
V	N	E	A	R	W	A	X	O	H	D	P
E	X	O	L	S	C	E	O	T	Y	C	R
O	A	G	L	I	N	T	B	F	M	I	R
I	K	R	I	A	H	U	A	A	E	N	I
N	T	O	N	P	D	M	S	C	S	N	K
G	O	B	A	C	U	E	I	O	Z	A	A
L	O	S	V	G	A	R	L	I	C	M	A
U	T	A	K	S	L	I	A	N	E	O	T
E	V	N	I	M	U	C	U	S	X	N	P
C	I	N	N	A	H	O	P	S	G	L	M

GOOD STUFF

THYme MINT
TUMERIC VANILLA
Paprika CINNAMON
garLic CUMIN
basiL

BAD STUFF

GLUE Toenails
HAIR LINT
earwax COINS
SNOT TOOTHpaste

my arm. I found almost everything I needed, although I had to make a couple of substitutions on the fly. Like I couldn't find the phyllo dough for the spanakopita, so I bought a frozen piecrust instead. And I couldn't find sea beans, or remember what they were. I figured maybe I had meant to write C-beans, so I bought cannellini beans because cannellini starts with C. And I couldn't find gooseberries, so I bought goose liver pâté. Also the oysters looked scary, so I got oyster mushrooms instead.

I hauled everything home and got to work. I'd told my parents that throwing a dinner party was a school project, which was true if you looked at it a certain way. They were taking Lisa out to dinner, which meant I had all the space I needed to cook. And because my mom had been eating nothing but Ethiopian food for the last week, because that was what "the baby wants."

It was already 3:45, and my guests were coming at 6, so there was no time to lose. I had the recipes printed out and taped to the refrigerator, so I could see everything I needed to do.

I heated up some olive oil and started blanching the spinach for the spanakopita, while the oven preheated and the pie dough waited. In another pot, I got some onions cooking and chopped up the cauliflower for the soup. I was graceful and precise, my every move full of purpose. Maybe I was a natural chef. Maybe someday I'd be telling the story of my first dinner party to a documentary film crew, in the kitchen of my very own restaurant.

The spinach was nice and wilted now, so I grabbed the pan by the handle. That was a mistake, because the handle was super hot. I dropped it and sprinted to the sink to run some cold water over my hand. The good news was the spinach hadn't landed on the floor. The bad news was the pan had come down on the piecrust, causing it to flip through the air and land in what was going to be the cauliflower soup.

I tried to take it out, but the dough was melty from the heat. I thought back to a soup my dad had made once. He had used flour to thicken it up, so maybe this was okay—pie dough was mostly flour, after all. The spanakopita was ruined, but creamed spinach was actually something you saw on menus, so maybe I could just throw in the spinach and it would be a creamed cauliflower and spinach soup. It was worth a try. I added the rest of the ingredients: water, bouillon, the cauliflower, some spices.

I turned my attention to the massaged kale salad with apples and Marcona almonds, but there was a problem: somehow, in all the confusion, the recipe had gotten wet, and I couldn't read it anymore. How hard could a salad be, though? You made a dressing, you chopped stuff, you threw it all together. Voilà.

The massaging was the only part I wasn't sure about, but that seemed simple enough, too. My sister had some almond glow massage oil in her room, and since the salad already had almonds, I figured that would be just the thing to use on the kale. I ran upstairs, grabbed it, and boom—five minutes later the salad was done and sitting in a nice wooden bowl, all ready to go.

It was past five now, which meant I had to get my salmon ready. The recipe had tiny amounts of about fifteen different spices—a teaspoon of salt, a pinch of Aleppo pepper, a teaspoon of thyme, blah blah blah. I had to really focus to get all that stuff right, and I got so absorbed in it that I forgot all about my soup until smoke started billowing from the pot. I lifted the lid and saw something that did not resemble soup so much as a ball of greenish-gray glue. The piecrust had sponged up all the liquid—and then, because there was no liquid, the whole thing had started burning.

I didn't have time for this. I tossed the entire mess in the garbage and turned my attention to the beef tenderloin with gooseberry sauce—I mean, goose liver

pâté sauce, since that was what I'd bought instead, and which, I now realized, was a very poor substitute since liver and berries are nothing like each other. But I'd made my bed, and now I had to eat it. I was beginning to think that a bed might actually taste better than several courses of this tasting menu. But whatever. I stirred the goose liver into the mixture of lemon, sugar, and garlic that the recipe called for, and smeared it on the beef. It looked and smelled kind of weird, so at the last second I covered the whole thing in these crispy Chinese noodles we happened to have in the cupboard, to give it a nice crunchy texture, and threw it in the oven.

That was when the doorbell rang.

CHAPTER 9

I took one final look around the kitchen before going to answer the door. The state of the seven-course tasting menu I'd promised my friends looked something like this:

FIRST COURSE: ~~miniature spanakopita~~ empty plate

COURSE 1

SECOND COURSE: ~~cream of cauliflower soup~~ blackened inedible ball of starch/spinach/cauliflower served in a garbage can

COURSE 2

THIRD COURSE: massaged kale salad with apples and Marcona almonds

course 3

FOURTH COURSE: roasted wild salmon with ~~sea~~ cannellini beans and ~~oysters~~ oyster mushrooms

FIFTH COURSE: ~~grapefruit granita~~ empty bowl, since I never got around to making it

SIXTH COURSE: beef tenderloin ~~with gooseberry sauce~~ smeared with goose liver pâté, crunchy noodles, and other random ingredients

SEVENTH COURSE: ~~apple pie and homemade bacon ice cream~~ half a carton of mint peanut butter ice cream, which is freezer-burned because nobody in my family likes it, so it's been in the freezer for "emergencies" since I was five. Except that there was only a tiny bit left, because my mom has been having pregnancy cravings and apparently she devoured nine-tenths of the carton sometime in the last few weeks.

I opened the door and found Azure, Forrest, Klaus, Bin-Bin, and Bailey standing there. Forrest was holding

a bouquet of wildflowers that he'd probably picked on his farm, and Bailey had a bottle of sparkling apple juice.

"Welcome to Chez Jake! I hope you brought your appetites," I said, although secretly I hoped they had stopped for a pizza on the way over.

"Oh, yeah," said Azure, raising one eyebrow at me. "I can't wait to taste the latest flavors of my favorite chef."

"Same here," said Bailey, handing me the apple juice.

I showed them all in and sat them down at the table. "Here's the first course," I said. "Massaged kale salad with apples and Marcona almonds." If I was lucky, maybe they'd fill up on salad, and I wouldn't have to serve anything else.

"Yum," said Bin-Bin. She took a big bite, chewed a

couple of times, then paused. "What is the kale massaged with?" she asked through a mouthful of salad.

"Massage oil," I said, taking a bite and immediately realizing that this had been a terrible idea. The kale might as well have been coated in motor oil.

"It's, um, an experimental dish I've been experimenting with," I said lamely, choking down my bite. Everyone nodded politely, and that was when I started to feel really bad. My friends were such good friends that they were willing to eat trash if the alternative was offending me. I couldn't let that happen. "I guess the experiment failed," I said breezily, and jumped up to clear away the plates.

"It happens," said Bailey encouragingly. "You wanna make an omelet, you have to break some eggs, right?"

"Right," I said thankfully.

"Omelet iz next course, Ze Dentist?" asked Klaus hopefully.

"No," said Azure. "It's just an expression."

"Rats," said Klaus. "Klaus likes a gut omelet."

"A gut omelet?" asked Bailey. "What kind of gut? Like cow intestine?"

"No," said Klaus. "Gut. Gut."

"Good," Azure translated.

"Yes." Klaus nodded. "Gut."

"No," said Forrest when I tried to take his plate. "I like it. I can taste the love."

"Suit yourself," I said, and carried the rest of the plates into the kitchen.

I peered into the oven. The goose liver pâté sauce had turned crusty and brown. I might as well call this dish beef with dog poop sauce.

I tasted the salmon. Something was definitely not right. It took me a second, but I figured out what it was: I had used sugar instead of salt. And a tablespoon instead of a teaspoon. And cayenne pepper instead of paprika. And another tablespoon instead of a teaspoon. In other words, this dish was basically turning out to be salmon-flavored too-sweet-and-spicy-to-eat mess.

I looked around my food-spattered, smoke-filled, foodless kitchen in desperation.

That was when inspiration struck. I picked up the phone and called Evan.

"Hello?" he said, except it sounded more like "Hwwmmf?" which probably meant that Evan was stuffing his face as usual.

"Dude," I said, "stop stuffing your face as usual. I need a giant favor."

"You got a lot of nerve, The Dentist. My hair hasn't even grown back yet, and you already need something else? Let me guess—you told Bailey you're an expert eyebrow trimmer and now you wanna shave off my eyebrows."

"It's nothing like that," I said. "I'm in a jam because my seven-course tasting menu is basically seven flavors of garbage. I need you to bring over a whole bunch of Chinese food. Like ten cartons' worth."

Evan thought about that for a second. I could hear him chewing. "From the good place or the cheap place?"

"The cheap place. They're quicker, and I don't have a lot of time. And I need you to bring it to the kitchen door, okay?"

Evan chewed for a couple more seconds, then said, "Don't tell me you're going to try to pass Lucky Wah off as your own cooking."

"I'm gonna try," I said, and hung up.

I had to do something to pass the time until Evan arrived, so I decided to serve my guests a palate cleanser. This is a thing they do between courses in super-fancy restaurants, to get the last taste out of your mouth so the next taste can go in. It's usually a little dainty spoonful of grapefruit sorbet or something like that, but I had to make do with what I had.

MONTY'S PALATE CLEANSING

SCRAPE SCRAPE SCRUB SCRUB

"Here we go," I called out, striding into the dining room with five bowls balanced on a tray. "A little palate cleanser before the savory courses."

Bailey tasted hers. "Interesting palate cleanser," she said. "Is this peanut butter mint ice cream?"

Azure crinkled up her nose. "It tastes kind of . . . old or something. Is it supposed to?"

"Of course!" I cried. "It's specially cave-aged for eighteen months."

"Cave-aged ice cream?" said Bin-Bin, and I cringed, waiting for her to say something like "That's the most

ridiculous thing I've ever heard in my life." But instead she just shrugged and said, "Fancy."

"You can really taste the cavey-ness," Forrest said, wolfing his down like he hadn't been fed in weeks. He glanced over at Azure's and Bailey's barely touched bowls, and without a word they both slid theirs over to him, like some kind of Olympic synchronized bowl-passing team.

Just then, I heard a faint tap-tapping at the kitchen door, and I leapt up to go let Evan in, shouting, "Be right back with our main courses!" over my shoulder as I went.

Evan was loaded down with so many boxes and containers he could hardly see over them. I started unpacking as fast as I could: spring rolls, beef with broccoli, sweet and sour soup, spicy chicken with cashews, Szechuan string beans. I plated everything— except the soup, which I bowled (which sounds like I rolled it at a bunch of pins, I know, but I'm not sure what else to say).

"Thanks, dude," I whispered to Evan.

"No sweat," he said, piling a serving platter with food for himself. "I was in the mood for a second dinner anyway. Also, you owe me a hundred and twenty-two bucks. Plus tip." He disappeared into my basement to gorge.

"Here we go!" I announced. "The main courses are served. I decided to do a kind of pan-Chinese menu tonight. Here we have my take on sweet and sour soup, from the Hunan province. These are Szechuan green beans, a classic recipe that I've, you know, kind of reinvented a little bit. And here's some cashew chicken, a twist on a classic Northern dish that I've added some Southern elements to. And here we have the beef with broccoli, which is more of an American Chinese dish, but hey, we're in America, so I figured what the heck, authenticity isn't everything, why not?"

CA-CA-

SHOO!!

CASHEW CHICKEN!!

FLORP!!

I had no idea what I was talking about, but all those nights of improvising with Maury had paid off. The words just flowed out of my mouth, and as far as I could tell, they sounded good.

Everybody dug in, and for the next couple of minutes, I was rewarded for my efforts with the sound every chef hopes for: silence. People enjoying their food so much that they don't even want to talk.

"Yum," Azure said after a while, breaking the silence. "I have to admit, Jake, I was a little skeptical after those first courses, but this is delicious."

"Klaus agrees," said Klaus. "Zomeone pazz Klaus ze zweet und zour zoup, please."

"It's all really excellent," said Bailey. "Especially the chicken."

That was when it happened. She stabbed a piece of chicken with her fork and brought it to her mouth.

There was something attached to the chicken.

A piece of paper. Bailey frowned and pulled it off the tines.

I knew what it was.

My stomach did a backflip. I thought about reaching out and trying to grab it, but I was too late.

Alien #1: Hahahahahahahahahaha! See? I told you this would be better than making him puke on her!

Alien #2: I'll never doubt you again.

Bailey looked carefully at the piece of paper and started reading. "Lucky Wah Fine Chinese Restaurant." She looked up at me. "This is a receipt."

Now the silence at the table was the kind every chef does not hope for: the kind that means your diners have just realized that you are a massive fraud and a complete schlemiel.

Then I had a brilliant idea. Maybe I wasn't a fraud or a schlemiel. Maybe I was an artist.

"Of course it's a receipt," I said. "I made sure it was there, so you would find it."

"Huh?" said Bin-Bin. "So you didn't cook any of this food?"

"Of course not," I said. "This meal is a ready-made. Like the work of Marcel Duchamp. And I deliberately put the receipt in the chicken to bring up the issue of appropriation. Like Andy Warhol."

"But you tricked us," said Azure.

"All in the name of art," I said. "Weren't you guys paying attention at the museum?"

"My stomach hurts," said Forrest. "I think I ate too much cave-raised ice cream."

"But ze ice cream iz not really from cave, yes?" said Klaus. "Zees eez part of joke."

"Not joke," I said. "Art project."

"I'm confused," said Bin-Bin. "I think I need more green beans."

"Can someone pass the beef with broccoli?" asked Forrest.

"This is the weirdest dinner party I've ever been to," said Bailey.

"Thank you," I said. "Thank you very much." But I wasn't sure it was a compliment.

RUN! RUN FOR YOUR LIVES!! THERE'S A FRAUD IN THE KITCHEN!!

CHAPTER 10

After the Ready-Made Appropriation Dinner Party fiasco, I figured I ought to get some advice from a true expert in the field of acting like a yutz, so I biked over to Maury Kovalski's house after school and told him what a buffoon I'd made of myself with the failed tasting menu and the takeout from Lucky Wah, and how at this point I was pretty sure I'd blown any chance of Bailey thinking I was anything but a complete tool.

Maury listened patiently to the whole story, nodding a lot and occasionally yawning or taking a bite of yogurt from the giant tub in his lap.

SWISS ARMY KNIFE

COMPLETE TOOLS

JAKE LISTON

When I finished, he stroked his chin thoughtfully and said, "Let me ask you an important question, sonny boy."

"Yes?"

"Is there any Chinese food left over?"

"I knew you were going to ask," I said. "I brought you some soup, some green beans, and some chicken." I took the containers out of my bag. "Want me to heat it up for you in the microwave?"

"Nah," said Maury. "The microwave is full of old magazines. I'll eat it cold."

I handed the grub over, and Maury went at it with the same enormous wooden spoon he'd been using for his yogurt. It might have been the only utensil he owned.

"Let me tell you a story," he said between mouth-fuls, "about when I was a young man."

"This was right after the Garden of Eden?"

"About five years later, yes," said Maury. "In Brooklyn."

"I didn't realize Brooklyn came so quickly after the Garden of Eden."

"Go back and read Genesis. Brooklyn was founded by the snake. Any more wise-guy remarks, or can I tell my story?"

"Sorry."

"Thank you. So, much like yourself, I was once an eighteen-year-old yahoo with a crush on a mysterious and uninterested girl."

"I'm thirteen."

"Whadda you want, a bar mitzvah? Hush up. As I was saying, I was eigh-teen, and this young lady, Rudolpha Smitz, she was my everything. My sun and moon. My burger and fries. My cheese Danish and . . . what are those things that go good with Danish?"

Rudolpha was my red-nosed reindeer!!

135

What do THE
DaNish call danish
in Denmark?

"VieNNese"!!

"Uh . . . coffee?"

"Coffee is good with Danish, yes. But no. The word I was looking for is schnauzer. I had a pet schnauzer when I was a kid, and I used to take him on a walk and get a Danish from the Swedish place on the corner. Why the Swedish made Danish, I'll never know. There was also a Greek place that made an incredible Italian sub. And a guy everybody called the Turk who was actually Scots-Irish. Now, remind me, pal o' mine . . . what the heck is my point here?"

"I'm sure I have no idea, Maury."

"Oh, yeah—so this girl, Rudolpha Smitz, she's into sailors. A lotta girls were into sailors back then. Sailors, you know, they were tough guys. Had anchors tattooed on their forearms and whatnot. So I say to myself, 'Self, if you wanna win Rudolpha Smitz's heart, you better make her think that you're a sailor.' Now, me, I could drown in a bathtub, practically, but here I go

Maury

Le French Sailor

pretending I'm a sailor so Rudolpha will like me. And the next thing I know, one thing leads to another, bada bing, bada boom, and somehow I end up spending six months in the French navy."

"What? Come on. You can't just accidentally end up in the French navy."

"Things like that used to happen all the time back then, boy-o. The world was a crazy place. My point is this: the most impressive thing you can be is yourself. And besides, lying is too much work. The truth, you never forget, because it's the truth. It actually happened. But with lies, you gotta keep 'em straight, and when you mess them up, you gotta invent new lies to explain why the old lies don't line up. And plus you gotta learn to speak French and deal with all the French navy guys making fun of you because of your accent, and also your propensity to get seasick all the time. You got it?"

I was pretty sure Maury was just making all this up, which would have been highly ironic since telling a giant lie is a very strange way to illustrate the point that lying is bad.

"Got it," I said. "Be yourself and tell the truth, or you'll end up serving in the military of a foreign power."

"Precisely."

"So how did you get out of the French navy?"

"I jumped ship in Bermuda one day. Earned enough doing stand-up in the resort hotels to book passage back home on a tanker ship hauling four hundred tons of Bermuda shorts to Florida. To this day, I can't even look at a navy bean—though I do still enjoy a good French onion soup—and let's be honest, there's really

no such thing as a bad French onion soup. All that nice gloopy cheese. Yum. Not too many soups have cheese, which is a real shame. If I was in charge of, say, minestrone, that would be my first executive decision—add about a pound of gloopy, gloppy cheese to that baby. Even in the navy, the French onion soup was not to be missed. Boy, could I ever go for a bowl right now."

"And what happened to Rudolpha Smitz?"

"By the time I got back to Brooklyn, she was married to a guy with a pants shop."

"A pants shop?"

"Uh-huh. Turned out I had misunderstood the whole thing. She wasn't even into sailors—she was into tailors."

• • •

Maury had a bizarre way of making a point, but he was right: it was better to just be myself. I guess this was the kind of lesson I was going to have to keep learning and relearning in life, because there would always be opportunities to keep it real or keep it fake, and I seemed to have a habit of choosing wrong.

If I really thought about it, though, all the people I loved and respected stayed true to themselves. Lisa and Pierre, for example. Sure, they could have tried to make music that sounded "normal," but where would that have gotten them? They'd be one of a million bands nobody cared about. Instead, they followed their own wackadoodle instincts, and here they were, drawing hundreds of people from Anchorage, Alaska, to hear them play songs about platypuses and schlemiels on a random Thursday night. Or take Maury: he wore a bathrobe onstage anytime he felt like it, and he told jokes because *he* thought they were funny. If you told him the queen of England was in the audience and suggested that she might take offense to his routine about how gross British food was, he'd look at you like you were nuts and then go out there and not change a single word.

My mind was made up: it was time to come clean. And so the very next morning, as soon as I saw Bailey, I ran right up to her and told her there was something I had to get off my chest.

I happened to see her in the school parking

SCRUB
SCRUB

PREPARING
To come
clean

lot, while Pierre was still looking for a place to park his Porsche, so in order to run up to her, I had to jump out of the moving car, which was probably not the smartest move in the world, even if the car was only moving about one mile an hour.

"Jake!" Lisa screamed. "What are you doing?"

"Sorry!" I yelled over my shoulder. "Hey! Bailey! Wait up!"

"Not cool, dude," called Pierre. "Who do you think you are, Usain Brolt?"

Bailey turned and waited. I guess I could have stopped running at that point, but I thought it would look stupid to suddenly break into a walk, so I kept sprinting until I got to her. By which point I was panting for breath and couldn't even speak, which made the whole thing kind of a waste of time.

She just stood there, waiting. Finally, when I could get air into my lungs and words past my lips, I said, "I have a confession to make. I'm not really—"

"A barber?" Bailey finished, raising her eyebrows at me and then waggling them up and down.

It didn't seem like the kind of thing you would do if you were mad.

"No," I said. "And also, I'm not really—"

"A gourmet chef?" said Bailey. I studied the expression on her face. She definitely did not look mad. More like amused. Like she was trying not to laugh—but like the laugh she was trying not to laugh was a really pleasant, kind laugh.

"You knew?" I said. "The whole time?"

"Of course I knew," she said. "Because you know what *I'm* not? A fool."

"But if you knew, then why . . ." I trailed off because 1) I was totally confused, and 2) finishing the sentence would have been too embarrassing: *Why did you let me make a complete oaf of myself?*

Bailey shrugged and grinned at me. "Honestly? I thought it was kind of cute that you wanted to impress me so badly. And I do mean *badly*."

I had to laugh at that one. Bailey was pretty funny. Somehow I don't think I'd really noticed that before, probably because I'd been too busy trying to prove to her who I was, instead of trying to learn who *she* was.

"Besides," she added, "I wanted to see how far you'd take it. I mean . . . I was considering telling you I liked to scuba dive, just to see if you were like, 'Coincidentally, Bailey, I just so happen to be the foremost leading expert on dolphins in the entire country, and I'd love to introduce you to some of my dolphin associates.' And then I'd show up and find . . . I dunno . . ."

"Probably Evan dressed up as a dolphin," I said, and we both started laughing.

RARE SIGHTING OF THE
EVAN-FACED DOLPHIN

HURRY UP!!

PORT -A- POTTY

"Aww, is it too late?" she said between giggles. "I'm dying to see Dolph-Evan."

"You're horrible!" I said. "You were just messing with me this whole time!"

"No more than you were messing with me!" Bailey retorted, and I had to admit that she was right.

"So . . . maybe we could just start over and be ourselves?" I said kind of hopefully.

"I'd like that," Bailey said.

I extended my hand. "Hi," I said. "I'm Jake. I can't cook or cut hair. I don't know anything about scuba diving, and I spend a lot of time hanging out with an eighty-year-old Borscht Belt comedian."

"Nice to meet you, Jake," said Bailey. "I think this could be the beginning of a beautiful friendship."

CHAPTER 11

After my talk with Bailey, I knew there was something else I had to do: come clean with my parents about the baby. I'd been bottling up my feelings, my worries, but I couldn't do that anymore. I had to turn over a new leaf—which is an expression I've never understood, to be honest. I mean, first of all, you could walk around turning leaves over all day, and what difference would it make, unless you're a caterpillar? And second of all, what's with the *new* leaf? Has anybody turned over the same leaf more than once? Is that even a thing? Like *Oh, yeah, for years I just sat around turning over this one leaf again and again, and it got me nowhere, man. But then—then!—I got this new leaf to turn over, and boom, since then my whole life has been great!*

That night was Family Sushi Night, and I decided I'd have a heart-to-heart with them as soon as the appetizers arrived.

My palms started sweating when I saw Sushi Bobby—that's what we call our waiter—coming over with the grilled eggplant and the seaweed salad, but I wasn't going to chicken out now. Which is another expression I don't understand, incidentally. What's the opposite of chickening out? Chickening in?

I picked up a big bite of eggplant with my chopsticks and said, "There's something I wanna talk to you guys about." Then I popped the eggplant in my mouth, where it immediately singed my tongue so badly that I had to spit it back onto my plate.

"Well, that was disgusting," said Lisa.

"Sorry," I said. Then I added helpfully, "Careful, everybody, the eggplant is really hot."

"Thanks for the heads-up," said my mom. She ran her hand over her belly, which was starting to poke out. "Now, what did you want to talk about?"

"Well," I said, "this baby. I mean . . . I don't know how to say this."

"Use words," Lisa suggested.

"Right. Okay, so . . . I mean . . . like . . ."

"Try some different words," Lisa suggested, and my dad laid his hand over hers, in a subtle gesture of *Shut up, Lisa.*

"I'm worried that this baby is going to change everything," I blurted.

My mom and dad and Lisa all nodded. "That makes sense," my dad said. "Babies do that. But what are you worried about, specifically?"

I counted on my fingers. At first, I was staring down at my spat-out eggplant as I spoke, but after a few moments I managed to raise my eyes and look at Lisa and my parents, one after the other.

"That nobody will pay attention to me anymore. That I'll just be some lame middle kid who isn't first or last or special. That

My original list of CONCERNS, edited for brevity!!

All-TIME
TOP 3
CONCERNS
about babies
WHICH NeVeR
eVeR CHaNGe:
• POOP
• SPIT UP
• Pee

SCRATCH
-N-SNIFF

I'll never get a decent night's sleep again. That I'll have to share my room. That babies are boring. That I'll spend all my free time babysitting."

My dad nodded. "Those are all reasonable concerns. Let's see if we can address them, shall we?"

"Okay," I said. Something weird was happening. I was starting to feel relieved, and nobody had even really said anything. It was like a rock that had been sitting on top of my chest had been lifted away. Just by naming my fears, it was like I'd cut them in half.

"So, let's go in reverse order," my dad said. "You're right, babies are kind of boring, at

CHOP
Fe
AR

CAN YOU FIND 7 DIFFERENT WORDS WITHIN THE WORD "FEAR"?

1. _ _ _   4. _ _ _

2. _   5. _ _ _

3. _ _ _   6. _ _ _

7. _ _ _ _

least at first. Not for the parents, maybe, but for everybody else."

"They're cute, though," said Lisa.

"You guys were kind of boring until you started talking," my mom said. "Then you got super-interesting." She ate a bite of eggplant. "It took about a year." She pointed a chopstick at Lisa. "You were singing at thirteen months." She pointed it at me. "And you were telling jokes at eleven. Funny ones."

"And before that, there are all these developmental things that are kind of cool," my dad said. "Like smiling, sitting up, turning over, learning to eat solid foods . . . There's something new happening every week, or at least it seemed like it with you two."

Why did Jake's parents change his diaper AND put him to bed?

Cuz he was POOPED!!

If age ain't nothin' but a numba—You're lucky I can't count!!

Baby Jake   Baby Lisa

"That doesn't sound so bad," I admitted, because it didn't. A year passed in no time at all. And maybe this kid would start talking even sooner, with me around as a role model.

"Now," my dad said, "as far as sharing a room, you don't have to worry about that at all. The baby's going to get your room. From now on, you're going to sleep in a hole in the backyard."

For a second, there was silence. Then we all started laughing at once.

"Your father is kidding," Mom said. "The baby will sleep in our room. At least until Lisa goes off to college."

"Or on tour," Lisa added. My parents ignored that.

"All right, let's talk about this whole tragic-middle-child thing," Lisa said. "And the thing about nobody paying attention to you. There's a word for that. I'm trying to remember what it is. . . ."

"Understandable?" asked my dad.

"Oh, yeah," said Lisa, snapping her fingers. "Now I remember. Stupid." She turned to me. "Have Mom and Dad ever ignored you before?"

"No."

"Have they basically attended every performance, game, and concert you've ever been a part of?"

"Yes."

"Including one hundred percent attendance at the Yuk-Yuk for every set you've ever done?"

"Yes."

"Same here. Including when *you* were a baby and *I* was the kid worried about suddenly getting no attention. Mom and Dad rock, Pukeymon."

Lisa had a point. "You guys do kind of rock," I admitted.

"We adult-contemporary rock," my dad said, and everybody groaned, which only made him grin bigger. Sometimes I think my father's brain has a couple of wires crossed and he actually believes that groans are the best possible response to jokes.

"Here's the thing about love," my mom said. "It's not like a pie."

"But it *is* delicious," my dad interjected.

"Hush up, Clarence. My point is, it isn't like there are only eight slices of love to go around, and right now you have two, but when the baby comes it's going to take one, and you'll only have half as much as you used to. It doesn't work like that."

"In fact, it's the opposite," my dad agreed. "The more love you give, the more love you have. Babies are love multipliers, not love dividers."

Lisa reached over and put her arm around me. "Get it, dummy?"

"Yeah," I said slowly. "I guess that makes sense. But there is one more thing. And I know it's silly. . . ."

"Nothing is silly," my dad assured me.

"Everything is silly," Lisa said.

"That's another way to look at it," he agreed.

"Okay," I said. "Well . . . I kind of feel like if the baby is a boy, I lose because then I'm not the only boy anymore. And if it's a girl, I lose because now I'm the only boy, and I'm outnumbered."

A sweaty ham is **ALWAYS** silly!!

Lisa toyed with a chopstick. "I have to admit," she said, "I kind of feel the same way."

"You two can't win for losing, huh?" my dad said. He glanced at my mom. She nodded ever so slightly at him, and a little smile curled up the left side of her mouth.

"Well, you're both in luck," he said. "We're having twins. A boy and a girl."

"TWINS?" said Lisa and I together.

"TWINS!" my parents answered.

"TWINS," said Sushi Bobby, arriving at the table with our rolls.

"Twins for the wins,"
my dad added, and he
and my mom high-fived.

"Can we name them
Batman and Robin?" I
asked.

"Absolutely," my mom
said. "Consider it done."

"Harvey and Edna," my
sister offered. "It's time to
bring those names back."

More TWIN NAME
SUGGESTIONS...

GReTel UND HANSeL

R2 & 3PO

M & M

SUNNY & SHARe

PORKY & Daffy

PoMMes & FRiTes

Pisa & LieRRe

"I like Valentina for a
girl," my mom said.

"That's beautiful," Lisa agreed.

"Your father has some strange ideas about boy
names."

"Hawk!" my dad said. "That's cool, right?"

"For a hawk," said Lisa.

"Two babies is soooooo many babies," I said.

"It is a lot of babies," my mom agreed.

"On the other hand," I mused, "that's a lot of people
for me to boss around."

"Now you're thinking like a big brother," Lisa said,
and slapped me on the back.

"And blame things on," I continued, realizing how endless the possibilities were. I looked around the table. "I probably shouldn't be saying this out loud, huh?"

"Eh, we probably won't even remember," my dad said. "We'll be so sleep deprived, we'll be drooling and walking into walls."

My mom elbowed him in the ribs. "That's not necessarily true. They might be good sleepers. Jake was a great sleeper."

"I like him better awake," my dad said, and stuffed a sushi roll into his face.

FUN & Fake FACTS about TWINS!!

JINX!!

EVERY TIME TWINS "JINX" EACH OTHER, A CATS TAIL FALLS OFF IN SWITZERLAND!!

!!!

ZZZZzz

NNNN

100% OF THE TWINS IN MAJOR LEAGUE BASEBALL PLAY THEIR HOME GAMES IN MINNESOTA!!

TWINS RECEIVE A 10% DISCOUNT ON BUNK BEDS IN OVER 120 COUNTRIES AROUND THE WORLD!!

ABOUT THE AUTHORS

Craig Robinson is an actor, a comedian, and a musician best known for his work in such films as *Hot Tub Time Machine*, *Knocked Up*, *Morris from America*, *This Is the End*, *An Evening with Beverly Luff Linn*, and *Pineapple Express*, and for his role on NBC's *The Office* and as Leroy in Fox's paranormal comedy series *Ghosted*. You can catch Craig in Netflix's upcoming *Dolemite Is My Name* and Disney's *Timmy Failure*. When he's not filming, Craig might be playing the keyboards with his band Craig Robinson and the Nasty Delicious. After growing up in Chicago and becoming an elementary music school teacher, Craig now lives in Los Angeles and performs worldwide as a stand-up comedian just like Jake (sort of). Discover him on Twitter and Instagram at @MrCraigRobinson.

Adam Mansbach is the #1 *New York Times* bestselling author of a picture book *about* kids but really for adults. This well-known work—whose title cannot be named here—has been translated into over forty languages and was named *Time*'s "Thing of the Year." Adam's other books have garnered such acclaim as the California Book Award

and are taught in colleges and universities across the country. He has also written a middle-grade novel about a boy who trades letters with Benjamin Franklin through time, and the screenplay for *Barry,* a biopic about Barack Obama's life as a college student. His work has appeared in the *New Yorker,* the *New York Times,* and *Esquire,* and on NPR's *All Things Considered.* Adam lives in Berkeley, California, and has three daughters, whose jokes would impress even Jake. Find Adam on Twitter at @adammansbach.

ABOUT THE ILLUSTRATOR

Keith Knight is the acclaimed recipient of the Comic Con Inkpot Award, the Harvey Award, and the NAACP History Maker award. He is the creator of the award-winning comics *The Knight Life, (th)ink,* and *The K Chronicles.* He is currently shooting a pilot for Hulu based on his comic-strip work. His art has appeared in numerous publications, including the *Washington Post, Daily KOS, San Francisco Chronicle,* Salon.com, *Ebony, ESPN the Magazine, L.A. Weekly, MAD Magazine,* and *The Funny Times.* Jake thinks Keith would fit in great at Music and Art Academy because he has stellar drawing skills and comedy chops. Keith lives with his wife and two boys in Carrboro, North Carolina, where they cheer on the Boston Red Sox, the Boston Bruins, and Borussia Dortmund. Catch Keith on Twitter at @KeefKnight.